"I want you to go ho_____ safe for you to go t_____

"With all due respect, Detective, you and I have some mutual interests here, but we don't have the same objectives. You need to solve a Los Angeles murder. I need to make sure that Tally is safe for all time. You're not going to do that and nobody else is, either. I'm the only one at the moment who can take that one on. I've got to find out who they are before they find out who she is, and I have no idea how close they might be."

"It's too dangerous."

"The only people who know my part in this aren't going to talk about it, so nobody knows who I am or what I'm after. I'm as safe as I can be, and if I blunder into something and get into trouble, I'll have only myself to blame."

———————————————— ★ ————————————————

CHANDLER'S DAUGHTER

TRULY DONOVAN

WORLDWIDE.

TORONTO • NEW YORK • LONDON
AMSTERDAM • PARIS • SYDNEY • HAMBURG
STOCKHOLM • ATHENS • TOKYO • MILAN
MADRID • WARSAW • BUDAPEST • AUCKLAND

CHANDLER'S DAUGHTER

A Worldwide Mystery/September 2000

First published by Write Way Publishing, Inc.

ISBN 0-373-26360-0

Printed in U.S.A.

*For Brendan, Carl, Ciny, Kelly, John,
Mark and Maura—the next generation*

ONE

I'VE OFTEN THOUGHT that the only thing really wrong with Boulder, Colorado, is that it is at least a thousand miles from any place else I might want to be. Oh, and the shopping here is crappy—but given my inability to develop more than a modest market for my software consulting services, that is of less concern than it once was.

Boulder is snugged up against the foothills of the Rocky Mountains and boasts the kind of community you might expect to find when a highly desirable climate and quality of life is coupled with a major research university—expensive. For that reason, I don't actually live in Boulder, but about seven miles northeast of it in an area called the Gunbarrel—so named, I am told, because, from a certain perspective west of here, the top of our hill is a perfectly straight line, or as straight as a gunbarrel. The name has an Old West ring to it that isn't borne out in the slightest by its appearance, which, except for the fact that you can see the Continental Divide from here, could be any suburban neighborhood anywhere.

I was brought here some ten years earlier by professional circumstances more than by choice, but I quickly came to love it. My only real regret is its remoteness from the friends I cherish, who are mainly now strewn along the two coasts, with a smattering slightly inland. There's another reason I don't live in the City of Boulder, the self-described "fitness capital of the world";

there's a rumor—to date unconfirmed—that people with fitness credentials like mine aren't allowed to live within the city limits.

Boulder also likes to fancy itself as "liberal," but its demographics show that it has little that it is necessary to be liberal about, being essentially a white, upper-middle-class city.

Anyway, it is a pleasant enough place to live in or, rather, near, and, at the moment when my story begins on the Labor Day weekend, had already been shut down for several hours.

When the phone rang just after midnight on Sunday—late for most of the people I know, but not too late for those who knew my habits—I waited for the second ring so Caller ID could tell me what it knew. It announced the call as coming from a local pay phone. I did a quick mental run-through of the list of people such a call was likely to be from and came up with zero entries, but I answered it anyway.

"It's not too late to be calling, is it, Lexy?" she asked.

I recognized the voice. "Don't be silly. I haven't changed that much in the last ten years. You're in the neighborhood, aren't you?"

A lot of people are still astonished by how much Caller ID tells you about them before you answer the phone, but she took it completely in stride.

"Yes. I'm at some place called the Gunbarrel Amoco Station and I'm on my way over, but I need a favor first. Have you got a garage I can hide the car in?" She was remembering my garage in basementless Palo Alto where I kept the things that Coloradans keep in their basements, leaving no room for luxuries like car storage.

"Yeah," I said. "You're only a few minutes away—I'll go out now and move my car out and leave the door open for you to pull in. Do you know how to get to the house?"

"Yes—I pulled a map right to your front door off my laptop two days ago. I'm on my way." And she hung up.

So she had been planning to come here for at least several days; why hadn't she let me know?

Tally Richard—named, her mother claimed, for that aged and much revered movie palace on the Upper West Side of Manhattan, the Thalia, where her mother and father had spent many an evening in their penniless student days, soaking up great old movies. Tally's observation about this was that she was glad they couldn't afford Radio City Music Hall. "Richard" was French in origin, and the family insisted on a French pronunciation, or as close as most Americans can come—"ree-SHARD." This tended to keep people from sticking an unwanted "s" on the end.

Tally had been my close pal through the decade of her preadolescence and adolescence and my advancing middle years, when I had been the tenant in the guest house behind her parents' house in Palo Alto. My friend Gladys knew Peter and Susan were looking for a tenant for their guest house to help them defray the costs of restoring their neglected Eichler. She also knew I was looking for a place to live in Palo Alto that I could afford, and so brought us together.

Eichler was the California architect who, in the postwar boom period, pioneered the concept of indoor/outdoor living with houses and townhouses with cathedral ceilings and glass walls that opened onto large patios. The area around Palo Alto and Sunnyvale is liberally dotted with Eichler developments, some of which are comparatively modest, others having more extravagant proportions.

Although it had been ten years since I had moved from Palo Alto, I visited with some frequency, and Tally and I kept in touch sporadically with phone calls, notes and cards on special occasions, and, in recent years, the occasional flurry of e-mail.

Now she wanted to hide her car in my garage. Well, that was fine with me.

I moved my car out of the garage into the driveway and anxiously scoped the empty street of my quiet neighborhood. As usual, Molly, my Westie, and I were the only ones not tucked in our beds at this hour. I had long since become used to the idea of being the only one awake in a world where decent people turned off the TV after the late news (which by my reckoning couldn't even be called late at the hour it came on in Colorado) and got up in time to jog before getting to work at seven. Tonight I was grateful for their virtuous habits. I had the distinct impression from my brief conversation with Tally that the fewer people who witnessed her arrival, the better.

In a few minutes a car came around the curve at the bottom of the block; I hailed it and waved it into the garage and Molly and I followed it in, closing the door on the still empty street as soon as the engine was cut. Tally got out of the driver's seat and we embraced. I probably snuffled a little, as I generally do on such occasions. She was dressed in jeans and a tee and a camel blazer, but as we hugged I couldn't help but note that the tee was silk and the blazer cashmere.

"Nice," I said, stroking her arm as we disengaged.

"Someone once told me that if it doesn't feel good,

it doesn't matter if it looks good, and I believed her," she answered with a laugh, referring to my fabric fetish.

We unloaded her few pieces of luggage from the car and stowed them in the guest room without any conversation beyond what was necessary to properly introduce her to Molly and to achieve the basic tasks of hospitality involving towels and spare blankets. This was a feat of self-control I wouldn't have thought myself capable of, but it seemed to me that I needed first of all to make her feel safe and comfortable before I got my curiosity satisfied. At last we found our way to our usual venue, the kitchen.

"This certainly looks familiar," she said. It resembled my kitchen in Palo Alto only in that there was too little space for much too much stuff. I have every kitchen appurtenance known to mankind, generally in multiple editions, and enough food stowed to have gotten Napoleon's army back out of Moscow. If the truth be told, I live alone primarily so I don't have to apologize for (or, for that matter, modify) the excessiveness of my habits—and my friends know better than to expect me to.

"What have you got to eat? I haven't had anything but airline peanuts since I left LA. They don't feed you on the airlines anymore. I guess that's what we get for complaining about the food. Sounds like something out of Woody Allen, now that I think of it." As she was saying this, she pulled open the refrigerator door. "Ah, here's something else that hasn't changed about you," she said as my overstuffed larder began a premature disgorging of its content; she caught the package of prosciutto just as it was completing its slide off its perch atop the provolone.

"LA?" I said, my inflection and eyebrow rising as one. "What were you doing in LA?"

"It's a long story."

"Here," I said, grabbing the package. "Sit down and let me fix you something to eat while you tell it to me."

And so she did. I started making scrambled eggs, which had been our staple late-night snack in those days when she would come home from a date and wanted to unwind and talk. Her parents, early birds both, would be dead to the world, but I would still be up and puttering around.

"You knew I was adopted, didn't you?" she began. I turned from the stove to look at her, but her face was hidden by the fall of her hair as she bent over to cement her relationship with Molly by administering a belly rub.

Her question, completely unexpected, caused me to stop and consider before I answered. "I suppose I did, now that I think about it. Susan and I never actually talked about it, if that's what you mean, and I always figured it wasn't a whole lot of my business, but I picked up the notion somewhere along the line." I tried to reconstruct the conversations over those years that had led me to that conclusion, but I wasn't able to pinpoint the moment when I knew. "You certainly seemed fine with it and I think I would have heard about it before now if you weren't."

"Oh, I was and am fine with it." She looked up at me with a smile. "Get back to work. I'm starving."

I turned back to the stove as she went on, "I couldn't have asked for better parents than Susan and Peter. I had the happiest growing up of anyone I know. And I've never felt any particular compulsion to know about my birth parents, which seems to be the fad these days. I suppose that makes me unnatural.''

"I don't know about that," I said. "We only hear about the ones that do feel that compulsion, not the ones who don't. No, you may be unnatural, all right, but that's not why." She grinned at that; we had both always maintained that we were both nuts, and that hadn't changed.

"At least it keeps you off tabloid television, and there's something to be said for that," I added.

"Well, hold onto your hat—I may just wind up there yet.''

"Oh?" I said.

"There's more to it than just that I'm adopted. There's some big mystery about it." She paused here, as if uncertain as to how to continue.

"Oh?" I was getting repetitious. "What kind of mystery?''

"Susan and I only talked about it a few times, but she told me the same thing each time—as if she wanted to make sure I understood—and it's pretty frightening if I let myself think about it, so I usually don't." She stopped again for a long moment, as if telling me would bring on the thing she feared. I simply waited for her to continue.

"She said the only way I could be safe was to not know who my parents were. That the very knowledge was a danger to me.''

"What?" At that moment, I felt a little shiver of fear myself.

"She said that as long as my identity stayed hidden, I was safe, but there were people who would hurt me if they knew who I was. You knew Susan. She

wouldn't have made it up.'' That was true enough—
Susan wouldn't have joked about something like that.

''She also told me that I was well-protected; that if
anyone looked into my background, they would find
documents that would prove I was Susan's and Peter's
natural daughter. And that the only people who knew
the truth would always protect me.''

''But she didn't tell you?''

''No. She said she would tell me the whole story
once it was safe, but it still wasn't safe. And then she
and Peter died.''

Susan and Peter had died together in a freeway
pileup almost five years ago.

''What's happened all of a sudden to bring it all up
now?'' And to bring you to me in the middle of the
night, I thought but didn't say.

''This,'' she said, bringing forth from her pocket a
crumpled piece of paper. I took it gingerly and opened
it up to read:

Friday, August 30

Tally,
I think you may be in danger. They are getting
close to the connection between PJ and SFR. I
need to talk to you. Meet me at the San Carlos
Court at 10PM tonight. Come straight to room
D106. It's in the last row at the top of the hill.
Don't go to the lobby and don't let anyone see
you.

SFR—Susan Franklin Richard. Tally's mother.

There was no signature; the writing was Palmer
method in its purest incarnation and told me nothing
about the person who had written it except that it was

probably a woman.

"Who's PJ?" I asked.

"I haven't any idea," she answered. "I have a funny feeling about the note, though—like I was supposed to know who it was from and what it was about."

"But you don't."

"But I don't."

"How did you get it?"

"The note was hand-delivered to my room at the Beverly Wilshire—slipped under the door—the day before yesterday. Friday, that is. I was in Beverly Hills for a conference all last week."

"I know the San Carlos," I said. "I stayed there for a couple of months back in the late 'sixties. I wasn't fancy enough to stay at the Beverly Wilshire, myself. Well, did you go?"

"Yes, I went. When I got there, the place was crawling with cops and when I realized that the fuss was about something in the room I was supposed to be going to, I hung around only long enough to find out that a woman had died there. I guess Susan had succeeded in making an impression on me, because I got really scared. I went back to the Beverly Wilshire, checked out, and drove down the coast until I calmed down and realized no one was following me. When I got to Huntington Beach, I found a little motel and crashed. Saturday I went out and got the papers but evidently the story hadn't made the last edition, so there was nothing in the *Los Angeles Times*. I just holed up in the motel all day and tried to figure the whole thing out. I didn't get very far. The evening news broadcast didn't say anything about it and the Sunday morning paper didn't tell me much more than I already knew—

the night chambermaid found her when she went to turn the beds down. Cause of death not determined, name withheld pending notification of next of kin, and all that.''

She sighed and looked down at her hands. ''The one thing I did figure out is that it probably all has to do with who I am. Who my birth parents are, or were, I mean.''

''Why do you think that?'' I asked.

''Well, the reference to Susan, mostly. I mean, that's clearly who SFR is. And if I am in danger, it can only be the danger that Susan was talking about. I mean, I've pissed off a lot of people lately—the job seems to call for that on occasion—but that wouldn't have any connection with Susan.''

She picked up the note and stared at it for a long time, as if it had something more to tell her that would be yielded if she could only concentrate hard enough. She put it back down, looked at me and sighed.

''Assuming it doesn't have anything to do with my DNA, I think I must be an heiress. There has to be money involved. No other explanation makes any sense. Susan and Peter certainly weren't in hiding from anything. Peter had a really high profile, at least in the scientific community, so they didn't think they were at any particular risk. And I know I was with them from early infancy, because there are baby pictures of me with them, so it can't have been anything from my own experience, because I didn't have any. The irony of it all is that I don't need or want anything from anybody.'' She shrugged expressively, and then went on with her story. ''But I couldn't simply go home and forget about it, so I decided to come here. I went on down to San Diego and got a flight out of there to

Phoenix. From there I booked another flight into Colorado Springs—if anyone is after me, I didn't want them figuring out I was coming to Boulder because they might make the connection with you. That's why I didn't call you on my cell phone. I didn't want there to be any record of my calling you. I know I'm being paranoid, but I think maybe I ought to be.''

She was now yawning deeply, so I busied myself with my cooking chores. I set a plate of scrambled eggs and toasted English muffins in front of her and watched in silence as she dug in. ''Boy, does this hit the spot,'' was the extent of the conversation until she had polished everything off.

She began yawning again and shuddering those deep, uncontrollable shudders of total exhaustion. ''This is the first time in forty-eight hours that I've felt safe; now I guess I need some sleep.''

''It sure looks that way to me; we'll continue this tomorrow,'' I said as I cleared the dishes and steered her to the guest room.

TWO

IT WAS CLEAR that a good sleep had restored in Tally some sense of well-being; we prepared breakfast together, prattling about inconsequential things, while my brain rattled back and forth over how I was going to get answers to the obvious questions without just blurting them out. Why had she come here? What did she expect or want from me?

We sat across the table from each other, she picked up her napkin, looked at me, and said, "I suppose you're wondering why I came here."

"Yeah," I nodded, "you could say that."

"It's simple. I need your help. I figure that the only way to keep myself safe from whatever is a threat to me is to find out who I am. I don't think that Susan's advice counts under the circumstances. I need to find out who is posing the threat and deal with it before they find out who I am and do whatever they're going to do. My gut tells me they don't know yet because, if they did, they would have had time after the death at the San Carlos to find me at the Beverly Wilshire."

"You don't think there's any chance that the death at the San Carlos was just a coincidence, then?" I asked, not believing it for a second myself.

"It could have been a coincidence, but I can't afford to assume that. The note was definitely a warning of some sort, and the person who presumably sent it is very dead. I think I have a slight advantage at the moment—because I know that someone is looking for me—and I've got to run with it, but I can't do it alone. I can't go nosing around in this without running the risk of exposing myself—for all I know, they'd recognize me at first sight. I have a sort of distinctive appearance, after all." I couldn't quarrel with that; hers was not a face you could fail to notice in a crowd. "I could be someone's spitting image. That's why I need you to nose around for me."

So there it was. I started in on all the reasons why I was the worst possible choice for this assignment. "I'm old. I'm fat. I'm lazy. I can't go up a flight of stairs without resting at the top. I can't stand in one place for more than five minutes before I have to sit down. I can't go more than an hour between pit stops."

When I had run through the entire litany of my physical and mental shortcomings, she dismissed all my objections with a wave of her hand.

"You're perfect. You've always said that no one takes fat old women seriously, so who's going to believe you're anyone to worry about? They're looking for me, not someone who is more than a quarter century older. You're familiar with all the background information, such as it is, and the places that have to be checked out—my God, you've even lived at the San Carlos, not that I expect you'll find my birth parents hiding under the carpet there. And if I recall correctly from your last e-mail, you have nothing to do right now. Both your consulting projects are on hold. You need the money."

"What money?" I said.

"I'll pay you your consulting rate plus full expenses starting yesterday—first class all the way and you can take Molly along, too."

"But I'm a software consultant, not an investigator. I couldn't take your money," I demurred.

"Oh, yes, you can. Even if Susan and Peter hadn't already left me well-fixed for life, the royalties on Peter's inventions roll in thicker and faster every year. The industry crystal-ball gazers assure me that the technology is going to be good for years, but I'd be more than okay even if it all ended tomorrow. Peter was a much more amazing guy than even we knew. Not to mention that Tally Richard is somewhat of a comer in her own right. I'm going to spend this money on someone to help me out with this. Why not you?"

"Well, maybe because I haven't the foggiest idea how to conduct an investigation."

She leaned across the table and clasped her hand on my forearm, saying with great sincerity, "But I need you."

I started to laugh and she joined me.

"Oh, that's really good," I said.

"Damn it," she said, "you still can't con a con artist, can you. I can't tell you the number of times this very gesture has worked with other people."

"Who says it's not working now?" I replied.

"In any case, I think you do know how to conduct at least this investigation. This place is stacked to the rafters with mystery novels; you go through two hundred of them a year. You must know everything there is to know."

She was right about the mystery novels, although I couldn't say the same for how much I knew. While there were many books on diverse subjects crammed into bookcases all over the house, my true vice was revealed in the bedroom, where the mystery paperbacks threatened daily avalanches off dresser tops and bookshelves. Of late, I had taken to having them shipped in by the carton-load—junkie that I was, I had to have a large backlog of them unread, to ensure that I could always find at least one to match my mood of the moment.

"Sure," I said. "Have you ever noticed that those guys go out on a single interview and immediately find the nosy old neighbor who remembers what he had for breakfast that day forty years ago when the victim disappeared and so he spills his gut and they go dig up the basement and find the victim's skeleton? Then he does ten more interviews all over the county with roughly equivalent results and then we find out it still isn't noon yet? And then the taciturn cop conveniently leaves the critical file on his desk while he goes to talk to someone else? And there's always a photographer conveniently around taking a photo of the suspect both before and after he loses the button that is found clutched in the victim's hand? And those guys *never* have to go to the bathroom, take out the garbage, sit down and pay the bills, pick up something at the supermarket, or read themselves to sleep. Sure, I love the stuff, but I don't believe any of it for a minute."

"Well, so what? I need you to do it for me because you're the only one I trust. And you've got to do it because if you don't and something happens to me, you'll never forgive yourself." That one was already pretty good, but then she lobbed the clincher: "And there's one more thing. Susan said if there was ever any trouble, I should come to you and you would be able to help me."

My face must have revealed the confoundment I felt at that point. There was no doubt that Susan and I had been great friends and would have done as much as we could to ensure each other's well being, but this did seem to go a little beyond that. "Well, Lord knows I would try, but—"

"No, she was very clear about that. She said you *would* be able to help me."

"That doesn't make any sense," I said.

"Oh, dear—I was hoping it would make sense to you because it didn't make any sense to me, either."

We stared at each other for a long time.

"The jewelry case," I said. It had dawned on her at the same time, and we nodded at each other in unison.

"Where is it?" she asked, rising out of her chair.

"On top of the armoire in my room. Bring it in here; the light is brightest here, and while you're at it, grab the magnifying glass off my desk in the office."

The jewelry case was a hand-crafted musical one that played "Zip-A-Dee-Doo-Dah" in a cheery tinkling tone. Susan had left it to me in her will, along with a knock-your-eye-out pink tourmaline ring I had long admired and now wore all the time. It took us only seconds to determine that the case had a secret compartment and quite a bit longer to find out how to open it. A spider had been there before us but had long since abandoned the territory for greener pastures. Now the compartment held a tissue bundle. I opened it to reveal a ring.

"That's mother's friendship ring," she said, "from when she was in high school. They were all the rage in the 'fifties. But wait a minute—it can't be mother's ring. *I* have mother's ring."

Friendship rings. The exchanging of them was a fad when I was in high school, although I didn't indulge, myself. In those days I was a confirmed nailbiter and the wearing of rings was considered a sure way of drawing unwanted attention to one's hands. That's probably why rings are the only jewelry I bother with these days.

I picked up the magnifying glass and examined the ring closely. "This is PJ's ring," I said, handing her the ring and the magnifying glass to see for herself. The tiny engraving said "PJ." Tally examined the ring in turn.

"Sure enough. I wonder who PJ is."

"It's a woman's ring, so PJ isn't a man. My guess is that she's probably your birth mother."

"I suppose if it is an heiress thing, that's the only reasonable explanation that ties what Susan said together with the note and the ring being in the jewelry box she left you."

"That's the only one *I* can think of, offhand."

"What kind of stone is that?" she asked, handing the ring back to me.

"I don't know. Probably an aquamarine, but I'm just guessing."

"This is all going to involve Westchester, isn't it," she said finally and I nodded. Susan and Peter had both gone to high school in New York's wealthy suburban Westchester County. If the ring indicated a high school association, it was most likely going to be a high school in Westchester.

"See," she said, "I told you you knew all the places involved." And she was right about that, too. Although I hadn't lived in Westchester County for over thirty-five years, I had spent enough time there over those years to keep current my knowledge of its highways and byways and shortage of good restaurants. I had even gone to high school there, but not in the same town as Susan.

"Much more of this and you're going to drag in Detroit," I said.

"So you can go back and wonder again that so many of you lived in such a small house? Not on my nickel," she said. Since Tally still lived in her childhood home, the spacious Palo Alto Eichler, she had been spared the experience of visiting it after many years and seeing how really small it was—and in her case it wasn't. In my case, on the other hand, the house in Detroit that sheltered me, my parents, and my four sibs until I was thirteen was probably no more than thirteen hundred square feet, a space that wouldn't hold me by myself today (unless of course I disposed of the results of indulging a life-long passion for buying books and fabric, the two things that lose ninety percent of their value the moment you walk out of the store with them). I had made this pilgrimage while still Tally's neighbor and she was recalling my relating the experience to her when I returned to Palo Alto.

For want of any place better to put it for safekeeping, we restored the ring to the secret chamber where Susan had hidden it. That somehow struck us both as appropriate.

I knew by then that I was committed to Tally's investigation, so rather than think about it, we spent the rest of the day doing the quickie tour of Rocky Mountain National Park and the Peak-to-Peak Highway, not yet as resplendent as it would be in a few weeks' time, when the aspen turn and streak the mountainsides with their gold. The weather, as is so often the case here, was simply gorgeous, particularly to my California visitor. While days are usually sunny in the Santa Clara Valley where Tally lives, the summer is spent in a perpetual haze—I used to maintain that a clear day was one on which you could see the clouds. So the crystalline quality of the Colorado air, coupled with the view of cumulus nimbus building up over the mountains in preparation for the daily lightning display, was suitably spectacular and appreciated.

Trail Ridge Road in Rocky Mountain National Park worked its usual magic. We spotted elk in the lowlands and bighorns on the high barren slopes above the treeline. We stopped to feed bread to the Steller's jays, who grabbed it from your outstretched hand as they flew by, and sunflower seeds to the tiny chattering pikas, who vacuumed them from the rocks into their cheeks before disappearing again into the crannied rocks to add them to their haypiles, stashed for those winter days when no tourists with their sunflower largesse could get up this far.

The Labor Day traffic was heavy, but not impossible. We had dinner at my favorite restaurant, Kim's Vietnamese in Longmont, and then came home to a double feature of Hitchcock movies to put me, as Tally put it, "in the right frame of mind." When we hit the cornfield scene in *North by Northwest,* I had to point out that there were limits to what I was willing to undergo, and when Grace Kelly started up the fire escape in *Rear Window,* I reminded her that I don't do ladders, but I was still committed regardless.

TALLY WANTED TO check that nothing untoward was happening in Palo Alto before she returned, so we had to wait until Tuesday when she could reach her housekeeper and the people in her office. It was afternoon by the time she was satisfied that everything was quiet and as it should be.

"It appears that everything is calm in Palo Alto,"

she said as she closed up her laptop. "No funny business around the house and no client uproars at the office. Steve can handle things there; he doesn't really need me except that I'm the boss and some of our clients think that is important."

"You were able to reach him on the laptop?" I asked.

"Steve's a computer junkie; you can get him on-line more reliably than on the phone, because he often routes his phone calls directly to the answering machine."

"Yes, I know the type."

"So where do we begin, Nero? Los Angeles or Westchester?" she asked.

"Don't Nero me," I said. "I may weigh almost the same as Nero Wolfe, but he had himself an Archie Goodwin to do all the legwork; all he had to do was the cooking."

"I'm sure he was much shorter than you are," she said, by way of atonement. "I can be your Archie Goodwin."

"No, you can't. You said as much yourself. You have to go home to Palo Alto and pretend that nothing has happened and keep your picture out of the papers. If anyone is looking for you, they may be able to identify you from a family resemblance."

"I guess that means I should stay off TV, too," she said.

"TV? Were you on television?" I asked.

"Yes, last week in LA. One of the local network affiliates did a piece on the conference I was attending and I was interviewed."

"Well, that explains one thing," I said.

"What's that?"

"How the woman at the San Carlos Court came to find you in Los Angeles instead of Palo Alto. I couldn't figure that one out, but if she saw you on TV and recognized you, that would explain a lot, like why she contacted you out of the blue and in Los Angeles, to boot."

"I hadn't even thought of that; the TV interview feels like it happened in a different lifetime."

"Let's just hope nobody else saw it and recognized you. You can't go anywhere near Westchester or even Los Angeles at this point. I'm not sure even Palo Alto is safe, except that there's nothing to indicate that they know who you are or where you live, or at least nothing so far."

We sat in silence for a while and then I said, "I think the easiest thread to pull on is Los Angeles. Anything that ties into Westchester has tied in for a lot of years now and will keep a while longer. Los Angeles ought to be the first focus."

"You just want to go stay at the Beverly Wilshire," she grinned at me. "You'd *love* the Beverly Wilshire."

"I'm sure I would, but I think the San Carlos would be more practical; besides, I'd miss being lulled to sleep by the roar of the traffic on the San Diego Freeway."

"Just what thread are you planning to pull on in LA, anyway?" she asked.

"Well, I have an old pal who's a screenwriter—does a lot of cop shows and true crime movie-of-the-week stuff. He lives in Pacific Palisades and I know he has sources in the West LA police precinct. I thought he'd be the first string to pull because he can poke around without my having to show my face. I want him to find out as much as he can about that woman."

"An old pal, eh?"

"Hey, I told you a long time ago that I had a misspent youth. You can't misspend your youth all by yourself. It ain't decent."

"Well, I'm glad to hear that you misspent your youth decently."

"Me, too."

TALLY HAD GONE back to Palo Alto on the last San Francisco flight out of DIA on Tuesday, and reported back that everything seemed to be quiet on that front. I was busy getting ready for my departure for Los Angeles the next day. In earlier years, I had traveled a great deal and prepping for a trip was routine, but it had been nearly a year since my last trip and everything needed checking out. This time, too, I had to accommodate my traveling companion, as well.

Molly eyed the hosing down of her travel cage, stowed since her puppyhood, with some alarm. But I had decided that she had better come along; if being a fat old lady is a good cover, being a fat old lady with a small dog is even better. Besides, we miss each other when we're apart, although I probably suffered more from it than she did.

Debbie, my once-a-week housekeeper, took in stride the sudden change in activity level as we sorted through my wardrobe looking for suitable outfits for undercover work in Los Angeles. "Mostly casual, but one or two power outfits in case I have to impress somebody," I had instructed her. We even threw in a pair of Ferragamos from my salad days, though if I had to walk very far in them, I was a goner.

Debbie only had one reservation about the whole undertaking, which I had barely outlined for her as a "confidential inquiry" about an adoption. I didn't tell her it was possibly dangerous because she wouldn't have let me take Molly with me if she knew.

"Don't you have to have some sort of license to do what you're doing?" she asked as she sorted through my underwear for me.

"Strictly speaking, I probably do. But I'm not planning to pack a rod and I don't think there's any rule against my going around and asking questions and looking at public records—they probably just don't like it if you get paid for doing it. It's not like I'm about to place an ad in the yellow pages—'Lexy Connor, private investigations.'"

"But you *are* getting paid for it, aren't you?" Debbie, realistically enough, was very concerned about my financial situation, given that her job security was seriously imperiled if my billings continued to be as scant as they had been for the last three months.

"Hmm," I responded, "let's just say I'm being paid for some very specialized software consulting and leave it at that."

THREE

WHEN I FIRST set foot in Los Angeles in 1962, it was still flirting with the notion of becoming the second largest city in the country and the aerospace and petrochemical industries were still the muscle men in town. In the nearly thirty-five years since, this "group of suburbs in search of a city" had stopped apologizing for itself and had cheerfully embraced its role as the capital of American pop culture. It still has its colossal front doors—its unique signature of a whimsical time gone by—but you have to know where to look to find them.

When I collected her from baggage claim, Molly was quite disgusted that Los Angeles International didn't seem to provide any private place for a ladylike pee and poop but in her usual unflappable way she didn't seem otherwise the worse for the new experience of airplane travel.

She was enthralled, however, by the public adulation that a Westie engenders among the female adult population of America. For those of you who are unfamiliar with the breed, the West Highland White Terrier defines "cute." Other breeds may be notable for their beauty or grace or intelligence or nobility, but when you're going for cute, a Westie wins hands down every time. So walking a Westie in a public place—and it hardly gets more public than Los Angeles International Airport—is inviting a chorus of admiration. We weren't to be disappointed.

I have long since lost count of the number of times I have breathed LAX exhaust in the passenger pickup area. The strength of the tourist business in LA is really amazing, given that they do their damnedest to gas visitors on arrival in this partially-enclosed car barn with hundreds of internal combustion engines running at full tilt as they jockey for curbside space and then have to jockey some more to get away from the curb.

As I struggled to contain Molly, her traveling crate, and my luggage in a single semi-mobile package while flagging down the Hertz bus, I was reminded once again how air travel had changed in just a few decades from an elite and cosseted activity to a mass transit cattle car operation. I could even remember when rental cars were actually picked up and dropped off at the LAX terminal. With much help from the Hertz driver and several fellow passengers, I was finally able to get everything aboard and stowed for the ten-minute trip to the Hertz lot—just long enough for me to catch my breath before we had to go through it all again at the other end.

The one area of travel that has improved dramatically in the last ten years or so is the service in the car rental business, so I was in my car and on my way up the San Diego Freeway toward West LA in minutes after hitting the Hertz lot. For some reason I have never quite fathomed, Hertz likes to upgrade me from my standard order for a four-door "full size" to their big white Crown Victorias—a muscle car often used by highway patrols and sheriffs' departments and, apparently, rarely by anyone else—so I often find people unexpectedly yielding the right of way. After Molly had checked the view for a few minutes and decided that one highway was much like another, regardless of the number of lanes it might boast, she curled up for her ninety-third snooze of the day.

It was still only late afternoon, so the traffic was not yet at its peak, which meant it was only heavy enough to strike terror into one's heart, but not so heavy that it had yet come to its usual stop-and-go rush hour state. We made it to the West LA area in good time.

The San Carlos Court had been drastically over-hauled—probably several times—in the thirty years since I had stayed there last, so while it was still a motel of sorts sprawled across a foothill landscape overlooking the San Diego Freeway, it looked to be, and was, a fairly decent establishment, tasteful and dec-orous, notable for its spacious residential suites with full kitchens.

I had asked for a room in the back, and was just turning away from the desk with the key to D118 in my hand when I felt a touch on the arm that held Molly in its crook.

"Ms. Connor?" I turned to find a heartstoppingly gorgeous young man at my elbow.

"Yes, I'm Lexy Connor," I said.

"Steve Raines. Tally sent me," he said, reaching out to give Molly's ears a scratch, thus endearing himself to both of us.

"You're Steve? But you don't *look* like a nerd," I said.

"Don't be fooled by appearances. I hid my pocket protector by way of disguise, but I'm an honest-to-God nerd."

"I hope you haven't been waiting long," I said.

"Not long, and it didn't matter anyway, because I carry my world with me," he said, indicating the car-rying case slung over his shoulder. "Are you ready to go to your room, because I have something for you and we need to go over it together.''

"Oh, shoot—after all these years, a man finally asks me again to go to a hotel room with him and it's because he wants to show me how to use a computer.''

"You got it.''

The room was much as I had remembered them, except that the color scheme was no longer predominantly pink, which I kind of missed. The room had evidently last been redecorated in the hotel industry's mauve-and-celadon period, with the usual color-keyed pair of paintings over the bed.

Once we had me and Molly and all our accoutrements disposed in the room and Molly walked in the area that the bellman assured me was appropriate for this purpose, Steve sat me down in front of an ordinary looking laptop, but I knew it was more than that.

Franklin, Richard, & Raines, Inc., built on the base of Susan's modest public relations firm, was ostensibly still a public relations firm, but the public relations was a front (a front that Tally pointed out was making a reasonable profit in its own right) for their real operation, which was super-secure and secret corporate-level computing systems for individuals. Their primary customers were business executives who, for whatever reason, wanted the use of a secure system that was not under the control of their usual computer staff, and independent professionals who needed the same level of computing capability as their corporate clientele.

This laptop was one of FR&R's special models which, when opened in the ordinary way, looked and functioned like any ordinary laptop. For me, they had loaded some garden variety word processor, graphics, spreadsheet, and personal finance software to operate on that side. However, when you opened the laptop in a specific way, which Steve now showed me, you were in a mobile computing system that silently communicated with a master system in their office in Palo Alto. All of the data was stored on the master system, none of it locally, so that even a knowledgeable intruder couldn't find any information on the local machine that you didn't want them to find, and no confidential diskettes had to be left lying around, either. There was a killer key that would hide the mobile system and mask it with the common system in case you were interrupted in a session; there was also one-and two-way voice communication, so if you wanted, any conversations in the room with the laptop running could be captured in Palo Alto as well. Steve showed me how to use its features one by one, but there were so many of them that I knew I'd never remember what they all did.

"Slick," was all I could say.

Steve grinned, "It's my baby. Tally figures out how to make money out of this stuff, but I get the real fun of designing and building it. This new modem is so fast you won't be able to tell the difference between working locally and working remotely. That used to be the one major drawback. Here, say hi to Tally." He pushed a key and turned the screen toward me.

Her response came back almost instantly: "I see you've met up with Steve."

I responded: "Yes, and I'm keeping him. He's smart, too."

And she wrote: "Not on your life. Buy him a nice dinner and send him home. Nerds love Chinese, so take him to Madame Chang's in Santa Monica."

"I guess we've got our orders," I said to Steve.

"Chinese sounds fine to me," he said.

"Okay, but let me make a phone call first," I said, dialing a Hollywood number. A familiar voice answered at the third ring.

"Wes?" I said. "Guess who."

"Holy shit, Lexy," he answered. "Is it really you? Where are you?"

"I'm at the San Carlos Court, just now heading out for an early dinner. Can we get together later?"

"Sure," he said. "Just tell me when and where."

"Nine-thirty. The cocktail lounge at the Beverly Wilshire?"

"I'll be there."

"Okay, see you then. 'Bye."

And that was our first conversation in twenty years. There had been letters for several years, and then they trailed off to the very occasional—just enough to sustain the relationship that neither of us seemed willing to abandon completely.

I HAD SOME TIME to kill after parting with Steve at the restaurant, so I drove around my old neighborhood in West Los Angeles, full of names now known to every American because of their connection with the most notorious murder trial in modern American history—San Vicente Boulevard, Bundy Drive. I wondered how the affluent middle-class personality of the neighborhood might have been affected by its daily presence in virtually every living room in America for two horrendous years. (This was still several months before Boulder was to have its very own grotesque murder bringing unwelcome international media attention.)

I finally crossed over to the wrong side of Wilshire Boulevard and slipped down a side street to pull up in

front of the dreary little apartment house that I had
once called home.

It had been new at the time, but had already held the
promise of future dreariness. Surprisingly, this neighborhood, a mixture of seedy bungalows and seedy little
apartment buildings built on lots that had once held
other seedy bungalows, was little changed. Even thirty-
five years ago I had wondered at the utter charmless-
ness of the place, but it had been cheap and my tightly-
pinched rental dollar was happy to find it. I wondered
idly what it rented for, but decided I didn't really want
to know. My life has landed me in a succession of
some of the highest rent districts in the United States,
and I didn't want to contemplate what this dismal place
might go for today.

My little pilgrimage done, I went on to the Beverly
Wilshire, where I was confident of finding not even a
trace of seediness. If any place in Beverly Hills can be
thought of as having class, it can only be the Beverly
Wilshire, which has that aura beyond what can be ac-
quired with just money. Of course, most of the people
who went in and out of its doors got there with just
money, and, more often than not, someone else's rather
than their own. But I was never one to be shy about
using expense account money, and it certainly wasn't
going to stop me today. I had abandoned the "dress
sweats" in which I had traveled for a navy silk blazer,
cream silk blouse, and flannel pants the color of old
ivory—and mercifully I hadn't spilled any eggplant
with garlic sauce down the front—so I felt perfectly
comfortable going into the Beverly Wilshire.

Wes and I air-kissed in true celebrity-talk-show-
guest style and I settled myself in the chair opposite
him. A waiter appeared instantly to take my vodka-and-
tonic order. Like many of my contemporaries, Wes was

sipping a Perrier-and-lime and pretending to enjoy it. Slightly too old to be hippies in the 'sixties, we had instead nearly succeeded in drinking the world dry instead. Few of us who had survived that experience drank much these days.

I studied his face for a moment—wondering at how boyish looks manage to age such that they can look old and boyish at the same time. I would have known him anywhere.

"It's good to see you," I said.

"And you. You're still my favorite fantasy," he replied gallantly.

"Still married?" I asked.

"In a manner of speaking," he replied. "As long as my participation in this filthy, obscene, unspeakable industry pays enough to support her living as far away from it and me as possible, she seems content to be my wife. She lives in Cape Hatteras these days. I haven't even seen her since Paul's second child was born three years ago. The only thing that brings her running back to my side is the suggestion that we might get a divorce. I learned a long time ago that if I wanted to be left alone, I shouldn't bring it up. I don't think she really objects that much to a divorce, either. I think it's just the notion that I might actually find happiness with someone else that she finds intolerable—that would violate our mutual misery pact."

"And are you likely to?" I asked.

"No. I have the occasional fling, but the women around here seem to find it difficult to love me for myself alone and not my golden contacts in the industry." I laughed at the allusion to a conversation of ours of many years ago, when I had lamented that no one loved me for myself alone and not my golden hair.

For the next few minutes, we caught up on a few other mutual acquaintances but that well ran dry fairly quickly.

"Okay," he said, "you didn't call me up out of the blue to chat about old times. What's going on?"

As quickly as I could, I outlined Tally's story.

He stared at me for a long moment. "And only today I was thinking how boring life as an honest-to-God Hollywood screenwriter had become. Wow. Murder, or at least reason to believe there was murder. Money, maybe. Long-lost child. It's got everything except a life-threatening disease, and we can always throw one of those in. Hey, if there's a movie in this, it's mine."

"Of course." At the moment, I wasn't going to speculate on how overjoyed Tally might be to be the subject of a TV movie.

"And you want me to...?" He paused for me to complete the sentence.

"I want you to use your police contacts—see, I don't love you for yourself alone, either."

"As long as you aren't looking for a starring part in a series pilot, I can live with it."

"I want you to find out who the woman at the San Carlos was and what happened there."

"Hmm. The San Carlos. That would be the West LA precinct that caught that one. I think I can do that," he nodded. "I'll try to get to see Bruce tomorrow."

"The cop's name is Bruce? You'll have to change that for the movie."

"No, I won't," he laughed. "It's Bruce Morita. He's Japanese. But I am going to have to eat sushi with him for this and you know how hard that is for a country boy from West Texas.''

Despite his long list of credits, Wes still believed that someday they were going to unmask him as a fraud and send him back to West Texas with his tail between his legs—in his heart of hearts, he wanted to have been a native New Yorker. According to him, this fear helped him keep his edge.

"Can I reach you at the San Carlos?"

"No," I answered, "call my cell phone. Here's the number. I don't know where I'll be during the day." Tally had given me her cell phone because mine still required that you have a car attached to it or recharge the batteries every fifteen minutes.

Wes and I spent another couple of hours bringing each other up to date on our current lives, his children and their children, my career and his. He was mostly in demand these days as a script doctor, but still wrote the occasional original script. "I've stopped thinking about being the Texas version of Paddy Chayefsky," he confessed. "They don't exist any more."

I've long held the opinion that the reason we don't have better writing (and perhaps better directing as well, but I'm not as comfortable being a critic of directing as I am of writing) is that the writers' names aren't listed as a matter of course in *TV Guide*. None of us know who they are, so there is no way for them to develop a following.

When we parted, the kiss this time was genuine, but after a second of unspoken mutual acknowledgment, we both decided to ignore the implications of that.

As I drove back to the hotel, I realized that I had just palmed off on someone else my first bit of information gathering; I began to think this wasn't going to be so difficult after all.

FOUR

As FAR AS Molly is concerned, room service is the best invention since pop-top dog food cans. Imagine someone's bringing all that wonderful stuff right to you and your not having to suffer agonies of anticipation while you wait for someone to finish cooking it. That morning I shared her enthusiasm. I've often thought that if sunny-side-up eggs, country sausage, and a Thomas's English muffin were not so commonplace, they would be considered among the great gourmet foods of the world. Of course, the chef has to treat them with respect or they come out as rubber, grease, and cardboard, respectively, but this chef knew his stuff.

I managed a chat with the chambermaid, who turned out to be one of those people who succumbed easily to Westie charm, and she told me I could leave Molly safely in the room without putting her in her travel crate and she would notify all the other personnel who might have occasion to come into the room. I also asked about "the excitement last week," but didn't get any new information except to learn that the woman had arrived only that day with one small overnight case and that she was middle-aged, polite, and nicely dressed.

By mid-morning, Molly and I were under way. It was unusually cool for September in Los Angeles—cool enough that I could safely leave her in the car while I went into places she couldn't go. The front desk at the hotel had obliged me with the address of the nearest public library, where I sat myself down with copies of all of the past week's area newspapers. I hadn't really expected to find much, and the search met my expectations. An hour and a half later, I had no information to add to what Tally had given me was that the victim was discovered by the night chambermaid who was turning down the beds—which I already knew—and had been dead for several hours. The reports concluded with the information that there were suspicious circumstances that were the subject of an on-going investigation. Still no name or address, but I was fairly certain that Wes would come through with at least that. I reasoned that the name and address had been released too late to be considered of any news value in Los Angeles. If the woman was from out of town, which seemed likely, her name would be news there but not here.

That done, I took Molly for a stroll in Palisades Park at the foot of Wilshire in Santa Monica while I pondered the facts I had at my disposal. It certainly wasn't much and pondering it didn't take long. Then I gave myself over to watching Molly explore a new environment.

The park sits at the edge of the world. To be precise, it sits on top of a palisade with a long, sheer drop to the Pacific Coast Highway below, narrow Santa Monica Beach, and the Pacific Ocean beyond. You have to be at the balustrade to be able to see anything but water.

Even on a slightly overcast day like today, the park was a beautiful place. You would recognize this park even if you've never been in Santa Monica, because it has been used in thousands upon thousands of movies and TV shows. Today it was crowded, as few things in LA aren't. But best of all, there were dogs around.

I neglected to check to see if dogs were allowed, on the principle that it is easier to get forgiveness than permission, but if we were renegades, we weren't the only ones.

While Molly thinks that people are pretty much okay, it is dogs that she really loves, and the bigger, the better. She was delirious with joy to find several large dogs to kiss up to—a literal description of her behavior as she stands on her back legs to try to lick their faces. Small dogs get the customary sniffing treatment, but big dogs are to be kissed. I figure that, in reality, it is some ultimate act of submission, but it is nonetheless entertaining to watch. Most large dogs are completely nonplussed by, but tolerant of, this kind of attention.

We shared the lunch the hotel had provided for us, along with some Brie and crackers retrieved from the minibar. Brie is Molly's favorite food. Although she knows that sharing food means sitting quietly and waiting attentively until a morsel is offered, the presence of Brie brings forth the tiniest of whines and a continuous quiver of anticipation.

No call yet from Wes, so at last it was time to indulge my vices, or at least one of them. I pointed the car east and headed inland. Los Angeles boasts one of the handful of truly great fabric stores in the United States, and I had held off as long as I could reasonably be expected to; it wasn't as if I had anything useful to do.

IT WAS NEARLY four o'clock and I had just completed arrangements for shipping my purchases home when the cell phone jangled in my pocket. Since this was the first time I had heard it ring, it took a moment for me to realize that I was the one who was jangling. I must have cut a dashing picture, fumbling to get it out of my pocket, turned on, and answered. It was Wes.

"Got some interesting stuff. Where can you meet me?" Always the dramatist, he wasn't about to tell me anything interesting over the telephone.

"Wherever you like," I answered.

"Are you near Westwood? Do you know where the Chart House is?"

"I'm not far, and I know where it is," I answered. "How soon will you be there?"

"I have a meeting with a producer that I have to get to, but it shouldn't take too long. I should be there by six, but bring a book in case I'm late." Wes knew how I hated to wait anywhere for anything and knew I would go nuts on him if I didn't have a book along.

The Chart House in Westwood Village was hidden in one of the quaint little courtyards that pretended that Los Angeles wasn't looming right outside. Westwood Village, at the front door of UCLA, had been for many years an upscale community of shops and eateries supporting and supported by its immediate neighbor, the campus. In the early 'sixties, the first skyscraper, the Kirkeby Center, came to the neighborhood, and stood for several years in splendid isolation. Today, a whole squadron of skyscrapers (or highrises, as the locals called them) had assembled to dwarf the Kirkeby Center and clog and choke the village. I had been among the first office workers to tenant the Kirkeby Center, a long lifetime ago.

Inside, this Chart House looked like every other Chart House from Dobbs Ferry to Los Gatos, but the food was reliably good.

As it happened, Wes arrived only a few minutes past

the appointed hour. As he settled his books and papers and himself I kept asking, "Well? Well? Well? What'd you get?"

"First of all," he replied finally, "you have to know that Bruce wasn't the least bit pleased at my asking about this one. He didn't believe that I'd just picked it out of the paper as a possible story line. He finally let it go, but I know he didn't believe me. I had to assure him that I was a good citizen and if I learned anything that might have a bearing on this case I would let him know."

"Well, of course," I answered, "but we don't know anything yet. We only have some tantalizing notions."

"Yeah, that's how I rationalize it, too, but I'm sure Bruce wouldn't feel the same way if he had the information we have."

"Okay, so I owe you the TV movie and I owe Bruce the collar—what did you find out?"

"Her name was Dolores Miller, she was sixty-two years old, and she lived in Santa Barbara—here's the address—with her stepdaughter, Madelyn Cross, and the stepdaughter's two children. They're both widows. She left Santa Barbara in the early afternoon of the day she was killed, telling them she'd be back the next day. She gave no clue as to where she was going or why. Evidently, this was fairly unusual behavior."

"Santa Barbara?" I said. "There isn't any Santa Barbara tie-in."

"Hey, it's just where she lived. She could have been all over the place before she landed there, just like you."

"True. It's just that other people are supposed to stay put so they're where you expect them to be. Okay, what else did you get? What about the 'suspicious circumstances'?''

"She died of a heart attack, but it was brought on by something else."

"What do you mean?"

"Well, according to Bruce, it looked like an interrogation had been in progress."

"What is that in plain English?"

"Someone was beating her up, but in ways designed not to leave visible marks. He said it looked as if it had been done by an old-time cop."

"A cop?"

"An old-time cop. Look, I was talking to a member of the police precinct that's been under the closest and most critical scrutiny of methods and behavior of any precinct in the country. If they're super-sensitive, it isn't hard to imagine why. What he was trying to say was that cops don't do that any more."

Like most middle-class Americans, my brushes with the law have all been positive ones, where the police were competent, helpful, and respectful. We still find painful the evidence that such experiences are not universal.

"So Dolores Miller died not telling somebody something that that somebody wanted to know. That sort of eliminates any random robber theory."

"That's what it looks like to LAPD. They're calling it murder."

"Do you suppose that what she wasn't telling about was my friend?"

"Well, that's certainly a possibility."

"And do you suppose it really was a cop?"

"On that one I wouldn't care to speculate. But it certainly had Bruce's attention and it had him worried.

I'm still wondering why he even told me, but maybe it was to make sure I'd know down the road there was no cover-up going on. These guys are paranoid."

"Do you blame them?"

"No."

TALLY ANSWERED my call on the second ring. "I'm so glad it's you. I've been worried," she said.

"No need to worry. I haven't even stuck my head above the foxhole. The LAPD would probably like to meet me, but they don't know it yet." And I told her what Wes had discovered, neglecting to mention the TV movie.

Dolores Miller was as mystifying a name to her as it had been to me. "Do you think she could have been my mother?" she asked.

"I suppose that's a possibility, but the initials don't match. She could have changed her name. I'm going to Santa Barbara tomorrow to see what I can find out."

"Be careful out there."

"Don't worry, I will. Is everything quiet up there?"

"As quiet as it ever is. I had a couple of clients have minor hissy fits because I was out of town and unreachable, but that's pretty normal. And, anyway, the staff is perfectly able to take care of them just as well as I could."

THERE ARE faster ways to get out of Los Angeles headed north, but I've always been partial to the ambience of the Pacific Coast Highway, which I picked up early the next morning from the Santa Monica freeway. I had contemplated taking the rambling route along Sunset Boulevard to the sea, but the weekend traffic of the seaward bound was too much even for me.

Once we had shaken off some of the local traffic, that big old Crown Victoria stretched out like the Detroit land yacht she was and ticked off the hundred miles to Santa Barbara as smooth as silk—Topanga, Malibu, unlovely Oxnard and Ventura, Carpinteria, and then suddenly we were in downtown Santa Barbara.

FIVE

SANTA BARBARA. Only thinly disguised as the stomping ground of Lew Archer and Kinsey Millhone. At that moment, I would have welcomed the assistance of either one of them, since they both seemed better equipped than I to deal in old family secrets and their repercussions on later generations.

Santa Barbara is just far enough from Los Angeles to escape any implications of being a suburb and has a character all its own. Politically conservative except for environmental issues—an oil spill from offshore drilling many years ago had etched itself in the community psyche—it is a very pretty and a very wealthy community.

The Santa Barbara of legend has two parts—the sweep from Highway 101 down to the sea, full of houses that fall just short of mansionhood, set back in wide lawns on go-nowhere streets, and the hills west of the city that held the ranchos of retired presidents of various descriptions and people like that. The address I was seeking was in between these two, on the gentle slope between 101 and the foothills. It was a sedate middle-class neighborhood of single-family homes on modest lots. The house itself was a Craftsman, one of those salt-of-the-earth one-story homes that were built around the turn of the century from California eastward, at least as far as Denver, where they can be found in abundance on the side streets off Seventh Street.

This house reminded me of the house, probably to be found within a few blocks of this one, that my great aunt Ivy had lived in until her death at ninety-two. She had come to Southern California in 1904 with plans to die of the tuberculosis that had had her hospitalized in Richmond, Indiana, for the two years before. Being naturally perverse, she had instead become a successful businesswoman in a day when such were rare, owning and operating an office supply store in Santa Barbara for nearly half a century. She was already well into her seventies when I first met her, and described herself as a "tough old bird." I never doubted that for a moment.

I was about to pull the car into the curb in front of the house when paranoia seized me. I was perhaps about to make the connection that no one else had made between Tally and Dolores Miller, and this could be very dangerous. I kept on going up the street and turned at the next corner to head back toward the beach. I parked the car in the lot of the venerable Santa Barbara Inn, tucked Molly under my arm, strolled through the lobby and asked the doorman to get me a cab. I would arrive as an anonymous cab passenger, not with an easily traced rental car.

An aging golden retriever lounged in the front yard and began thumping its tail as Molly and I got out of the cab. It eventually rose to greet us in true I-love-the-world-and-everyone-in-it-but-you-most-of-all gol-die style. Molly did her kissing routine and the goldie seemed to think it was cute, too. Up on the porch the front door was open and I could hear the sounds of a TV coming from the back. A young woman with a baby on her hip and a toddler attached to the hem of her skirt came from deep within at my knock.

"Mrs. Cross?" I asked.

"Yes." She looked to be in her early twenties.

"I'm sorry to intrude, but I was hoping I might speak to you for a few minutes about your stepmother."

A dark look crossed her pleasant features. "It seems there are more people interested in her dead than were ever interested in her alive."

"I expect that may be so, and the only reason I think you would want to talk to me is that I may hold the key to who was responsible for her death."

"Who are you?" she asked.

"My name is Lexy Connor, but I don't expect that to mean anything to you. Your stepmother was most likely a friend of a friend of mine, but my friend is dead, too, so I can't ask her about it. I'm here on behalf of my friend's daughter."

"And what do you want from me?"

"I think your stepmother probably died because she was keeping a secret, a very old secret. What I need to find out now is who it was she was keeping the secret from. And before that person does anything to anyone else."

"You think she was killed?"

"Well, I understand the Los Angeles police think it's likely."

"They didn't tell me that. They just said it was suspicious and they were investigating."

"I don't think they like to say something like that, especially to the family, until they're sure."

"I don't like this at all," she said, "but, then, I haven't liked anything that's happened since Dolly said she was going to LA last week."

I think it was the fact that bad guys don't generally show up with Westies in tow that ultimately persuaded her to talk to me. Without saying anything more, she opened the screen door to admit me and both dogs. The toddler started to coo at Molly.

She showed me into the living room, dark by comparison with the modern California houses built since the end of the war, but nonetheless inviting and still cool despite the rising heat of the day. She put the infant in a playpen and the toddler obligingly climbed in after. I tried to remember when I had last seen a playpen used for children rather than puppies, but I couldn't. They seemed to have gone out of fashion while I wasn't looking.

We sat down and the dogs settled at our feet (Molly on top of mine) in cheerful camaraderie.

I wasn't quite sure where to begin, so I just plunged in. "Did Mrs. Miller tell you why she was going to Los Angeles?"

"Oh, please, call her Dolly. Nobody ever called her anything but Dolly."

"Okay, do you know who Dolly was going to see?"

"No, I didn't even know she was going to see someone."

"She sent a note to my friend's daughter asking her to come to the San Carlos late that evening. When she got there, Dolly was already dead."

"Did your friend's daughter know Dolly?"

"No. She didn't even know who Dolly was or why she wanted to meet her; she wouldn't have gone at all, except that the note mentioned her mother."

"And who was that?"

"Someone Dolly knew a long time ago, I think. I'd rather not tell you who she is because that was Dolly's secret and the more people who know it, the more dangerous it is."

"I don't know why she went to LA. I just assumed

it was the phone call again. She'd been to LA on Tuesday and was pretty upset when she came back. Then we were watching the news on Thursday evening and she suddenly jumped up and starting pacing around the room—it wasn't like Dolly to do that. Then she announced she was going to Los Angeles again the next day and would be spending the night. She never spent the night before that I can remember.''

Tally had been in the business news broadcast on Thursday.

"She went to LA often?" I asked.

"The twenty-seventh of every month, like clockwork, ever since I've known her. I would go with her lots of the time and we'd go shopping. Then, at five o'clock, wherever we were, she'd take a huge pile of coins and head for the nearest phone booth and be in there for half an hour to an hour every time. She'd been doing it for years. My father used to go with her when he was alive, and he was the one responsible for making sure that she had plenty of change for the phone.''

"Who was she calling?"

"I asked my father once and he said, 'It has to do with her family and she doesn't like to talk about it. You mustn't ever ask her about it.' It was so much a part of the routine around here that I just stopped thinking about it a long time ago." She ran her hands through her hair and looked at me. "It is pretty strange when you think about it, isn't it."

"Dolly was keeping a very important secret. If she went to LA to make phone calls from phone booths, it was so the people she was calling couldn't trace where she lived." And I wondered, had she not even told her family where she was?

"What could she have been so afraid of?" she asked.

"Well, she could have been afraid of exactly what happened," I replied. "The police think she was being interrogated when she died."

"Interrogated? All they told me was that the circumstances were suspicious. Poor Dolly—I can't bear to think of it." She got up abruptly and went to stare out the window into the street. I waited for her to get her emotions under control. She finally turned back to the room and sat down again.

"What else do you want to know?"

"Tell me who else has been interested in Dolly."

"The Santa Barbara police came a couple of times, and just two days ago there was an older man who said he was with the LA police, but I didn't think he was."

Old cop? "Omigod," I said involuntarily. When she looked at me, I went on, "There's a possibility that he's the one who was with your mother when she died. What did he want?"

"He wanted to know about her past. Where she had come from and when, what her maiden name was, stuff like that. Frankly, I didn't know that much about her; she never talked about her past."

"Would you tell me what you told him?" I asked.

"Her name was Dolly—Dolores, that is—Buchner, and she came to Santa Barbara in the late 'seventies. That's when she met my dad; they were married about fifteen years ago. She was a terrific stepmother; I don't know how I'm going to survive without her." She began to cry. I waited while she collected herself again.

"I'm sorry," she said, "but this has been one hell of a year." Looking at the baby, I suddenly realized that her widowhood had to be of recent vintage, too, and I was overwhelmed with sorrow for her.

"Don't apologize for anything," I said, "you have every right to be upset by all this."

"Well, right now I'm mostly angry—angry that Dolly didn't tell me what was going on so I could have helped her—and now, if you're right that her killer was standing here in front of me just two days ago, I'm furious that I didn't shoot him on sight."

"I don't know that he's her killer. I'm only guessing. And we might get our chance at him yet. What else did you tell him?"

"That she had come here from up north somewhere around Gilroy."

"Garlic Gilroy?"

"Yeah." Most of the garlic consumed in the US is farmed within hailing distance of Gilroy, a California farm community a few miles south of San Jose. During harvest season, with the wind just right, the whole Santa Clara Valley is re-apprised of this fact.

"Do you know where she came from before she got to Gilroy?"

"That's what he wanted to know; he kept hinting that she was from back east somewhere. If she was, I certainly didn't know about it. It's hard to think of Dolly as having a mysterious past, but then she never did talk about it, either. And I guess I was just too busy with my own life to ask any questions. I couldn't tell him anything, and I didn't like him anyway so I probably wouldn't have even if I could."

"Have you told the Santa Barbara police about him?"

"Yes. That's the main reason I think he wasn't from LAPD. After he left, I got to feeling really uncomfortable about him, so I called the officer who'd come to see me before. He seemed to think it was pretty irregular for an LA cop to come here to question me without at least letting them know. Up to now, all the questioning has been from them at the request of LAPD.''

"Questioning?"

"Well, yes. The first time they came was to tell me what had happened and to ask if I knew who Dolly was going to meet—and obviously, although they were very polite about it, to find out where I was when she died. The second time they came, they wanted to know if she had any enemies or anything like that. I didn't know she had a mysterious past and they didn't ask, anyway. I mean, who could imagine all this stuff came down because of old secrets?''

I was thinking to myself that I needed to talk to Tally. The name Dolores Miller might not mean anything to her, but Dolly Buchner might. And I was beginning to wonder how a real detective would go about finding twenty-year-old traces of a Dolly Buchner in Gilroy. And there sure wasn't going to be any Beverly Wilshire to stay in in Gilroy. Probably not even a San Carlos Court.

She interrupted my train of thought. "I just realized that there is someone who would probably know about Dolly's past.''

"Who?"

"Flora Snowden. When Dolly first came here, she worked for Flora as a sort of housekeeper and nursemaid. It was Flora's husband who introduced my dad to Dolly. I've always had the impression that Flora and Dolly might have gone way back together.''

I brightened at this. Maybe, just maybe, I could bypass the Gilroy experience. "Did you tell the man who came on Thursday about Flora Snowden?'' I asked.

"No, I just thought of her this very moment. She came to the funeral on Wednesday, but I only spoke to her for a moment.''

As if grateful to have something specific to do, Madelyn went to the phone and within a few minutes had gotten Mrs. Snowden to agree to speak to me. Since Madelyn had errands to run anyway, she insisted on driving us to the Snowden house. Off we went, this time to the western side of Highway 101 and the mini-estates with palm trees planted in vast green lawns.

SIX

LIKE ITS NEIGHBORS, the Snowden house was an imposing version of the mission style that dominates Santa Barbara's architecture. Madelyn dropped us off with my promise that I would tell her everything I knew once it was safe to do so and a number she could use if she needed to leave a message for me.

When Molly and I hit the front doorstep, we were greeted with deep barking on the other side of the door. Just to be on the safe side, I picked Molly up and balanced her on my hip. The door was opened by a Hispanic maid who shushed and downed the two gorgeous Rottweilers at her side. They obeyed instantly, although their fascination with Molly was evident.

"Don't worry about them. They're gentle as lambs."

"Even so," I said, "I'll bet nobody hassles them."

"No, they don't." She laughed as she opened the door and ushered us in. "Mrs. Snowden is expecting you; she'll be down in a few moments. Would you wait in the living room, please?"

The Rotties now disposed themselves by the door to the living room and seemed content to just watch.

The room was bright and beautifully put together. It was done in exquisite taste and orchestrated to perfection, but it was still perfectly obviously a family living room with books and magazines and notepads and pencils where one would like to find such things. The colors were light and yet warm and inviting—it looked like a room that had matured to its present state of loveliness and comfort rather than one that had been transformed intact from the interior decorator's sketch-pad.

I have an unreasoning terror of interior decorators, based, I have always maintained, on an experience I had had in the 'seventies. I had been invited to an engagement party by a friend of mine, to be held in his fiancée's apartment. The whole apartment had been recently "done" in the then-fashionable Chinese Modern style, even to the furniture in the bedroom of her three-year-old son. I was afraid to look for fear the dirty tissues in the wastebasket would be Chinese Modern, too. I found it simply astonishing in its single-mindedness and total lack of anything approximating comfort, but then I am fairly easily astonished at the tastes of many of my contemporaries. When I learned a few months later that he had come to his senses and broken off this relationship, I said to him, "Jack, you're well out of it. You would have wound up wearing Chinese Modern boxer shorts," at which he laughed so hard tears came to his eyes. When he had finally recovered his powers of speech all he said was, "Wasn't that awful!"

My approach to interior decorating is to put up the bookcases and then try, never quite succeeding, to fit all the books back into them. I maintain that having been a renter all my adult life has impaired my nesting instinct, but I never really had one to start with. If the chairs were comfortable, the tables convenient, the reading light adequate, and the colors unobtrusive, I was happy.

But I knew when I was in the presence of greatness, and this was one of those times.

With Molly still on my hip, I wandered around looking at the decorative pieces on display. This journey brought me to the piano, the top of which was covered with family portraits, some of them quite old.

I was idly glancing at them when I suddenly did a double-take. There was the photo of Susan and Peter that had appeared with their engagement announcement in the *New York Times*. Although they were much younger in the photo than they had been when I met them, the same photo had graced their mantelpiece for all the years I knew them.

It suddenly dawned on me that this picture and what it implied represented a link between Dolores Miller and my precious Tally; it didn't help me to find out what I wanted to know, but it could help them—whoever they were—to find out what they wanted to know.

She came in. Perhaps a little older than I, she was beautiful and elegantly groomed and coifed—one of those hairstyles that looks like it is no trouble at all and can only be created by an expert hand. I had to deal instantly with my prejudices about professional beauties (as in, "we could all look that good if we spent that much time and money on it," which of course we couldn't because it takes time and money *and* exquisite raw material); after all, a woman who could create a room like this couldn't be entirely self-centered.

"I'm sorry," she said, "but Mrs. Cross didn't tell me your name. You are?"

"Lexy Connor," I said, "I'm an old friend of Susan and Peter Richard's."

"Susan Richard? I thought Madelyn said you wanted to talk about Dolly Miller."

"She did. I didn't know about the Richard connection until I walked in here and saw that picture," I said, pointing to the engagement photo.

She looked a little puzzled. "Susan was my husband's cousin. But what does that have to do with why you're here?"

"Because I need to find out about Dolly Miller and the connection between her and Susan Richard."

"That's easy enough," she said. "When Susan knew I was looking for a housekeeper who could also take care of the children, she recommended Dolly, who was living somewhere near Palo Alto at the time."

"At the time?"

"Yes. Susan had originally known Dolly back east."

"In Westchester County?"

"Yes. We all grew up in and around Larchmont. What's this all about, anyway?"

"It's about Susan's adopted daughter and who her birth parents might have been."

"Tally was adopted? I didn't know that."

"Yes, and I think Dolly Miller died because she knew both who the birth parents are and who the child is."

"Perhaps you'd better explain this," she said, gesturing me to a chair, thoughtfully selected to be high enough and firm enough that it wouldn't later take a winch to get me out of it. "And you can put the Westie down; she'll be perfectly safe with my girls."

I realized that if Flora Snowden was going to be any help to me, she had to know the whole story, so I told her.

As I concluded, I said, "I've put you at risk now because I believe that Dolly Miller died because she knew that Tally Richard is the one who these people are after, and now you know it, too."

"I wouldn't worry about me," she said. "I'm well protected. There was a kidnapping attempt on me many years ago that was thwarted by our Rottweilers and now there are never fewer than four well-trained Rottweilers in the family at a time. I never go anywhere without the girls and the boys stay home and keep the house in order. People think real hard about messing with me.''

The Rotties thumped their tails at being the subject of our discussion. I've never quite figured out how dogs know when they are being talked about, but they always do. And any lingering image I'd had of a delicate lady-who-lunched died at that moment.

"There are four of them?" I said.

"Yes. We don't let all four of them answer the door at once. Two is quite sufficient for intimidation purposes and, besides, we like the idea of having some Rottweiler force in reserve in case anything does happen. Here, I'll let you meet them all. Okay, girls." Then, somewhat louder, "Okay, boys."

Hearing the release word, the two females by the door came over for attention, followed quickly by a thundering noise from the rear of the house as the two males came for their share. Molly was a little dismayed at being suddenly surrounded by a forest of dog legs, but once she was sure she was not going to be lunch, she relaxed and went about kissing all of them that she could reach.

"I assume you didn't tell all this to Madelyn Cross," Mrs. Snowden said, coming back to our conversation.

"No, I didn't tell her much at all. I just told her that I might hold the key to why Dolly died and that I was investigating that."

"And yet she talked to you anyway?"

"I guess she figures that anyone who wanders

around Santa Barbara carrying a Westie can't be all
that bad.''

"I wouldn't be at all surprised. And why haven't
you told the Los Angeles police?'' This question star-
tled me a little, because I wondered that myself.

"I'm trying to keep Tally out of it. I haven't wanted
to tell anyone about Tally's connection with Dolly's
death. My friend in Los Angeles knows that there is a
Tally, but he doesn't know who she is. I told you because it's more dangerous to Tally for you not to know
than to know. And there's reason to believe that
Dolly's killer is a policeman, which gives me more
reason not to tell the police. I'll tell them as soon as I
think they can make good use of the information. Madelyn has already told them about the man who came
to see her.''

"I think you need to tell them now.''

As I thought about all of the movies I'd seen and
books I'd read where all of the conflict could have been
avoided (and thus the movie or book, as well, which
often didn't seem like such a bad thing) if the heroine
had thought to call the police at the appropriate moment, I realized she was probably right, and said so.

The Rotties began to whine. "Okay, boys go,'' she
said and the two males took off as quickly as they had
come. "My husband is coming up the drive. Have you
had lunch? We're about to eat and I'd like you to join
us. I want you to tell him your story. After all, Susan
was his cousin. And he has lots of connections. He can
be a big help and maybe keep you from going to jail
for withholding evidence.''

I swallowed hard at that. I hadn't quite thought of it
in those terms.

IF YOU HAD CALLED central casting and asked for a judge, this was the man they would have sent over. He looked the part splendidly. And I knew him.

"Hunter?" I said.

"Lexy! What are you doing here? Florrie, you didn't tell me we were having company," he responded as he came across the room to greet me.

"I guess introductions are unnecessary," Mrs. Snowden said.

"Yes, we've met. We met at Susan's a couple of times—Lexy was Susan's tenant in the guest house for a long time back in the 'seventies and 'eighties," he said.

"But I never put it together. Madelyn Cross sent me to see Mrs. Snowden and I just didn't realize who Mr. Snowden must be. It's good to see you again," I said.

"And it's really good to see you. What brings you to Santa Barbara?"

"Dolly Miller's death," I answered, "and Tally."

"Tally?" he said.

"According to Lexy, Tally is adopted and there's some mystery about it that may tie in with Dolly's death," Florrie said.

Hunter sat down next to Florrie, across from me. "That's true enough about Tally," he said. "I found out while we were still living in Palo Alto, just a day or so after Peter and Susan came from New York. Peter came to me and asked me to help him in establishing an identity for the baby as their natural child. He said it was necessary for the baby's safety. Peter was a very serious and thoughtful man—he wouldn't have asked me to go outside the law like that if he hadn't thought it was justified. I had a couple of cronies at the university hospital and in the city and among us we were able to concoct a convincing paper history for Tally. There's a genuine birth certificate on record in Santa Clara County, with an attending obstetrician and everything. We were quite pleased that we were able to pull it off as well as we did. Those were easier times, though. It would be much harder to get away with today.''

"You never told me about it," his wife said, not quite petulantly.

"We agreed among ourselves that the fewer people who knew about it, the safer Tally would be."

"But surely the families and friends back east must have known that Tally wasn't their natural child," I said.

"According to Peter, they told their families that Tally was their natural child and the subject was closed and must never, under any circumstances, be brought up again with anyone. I would guess he made it stick. Peter had that way about him. They left New York without a baby and arrived in California with one, and Peter didn't think the circumstances surrounding that were the business of anyone but Susan and himself. There wasn't much family to tell, anyway. They were both only children and I think I'm Susan's only surviving relative. Peter's parents retired to France years ago and I don't know that they're still alive. As for the friends, Peter and Susan had just moved three thousand miles. In those days, people didn't hop on airplanes and fly all over the map for a weekend's diversion, so they just had to wait a while to let people know they had a child and be a little fuzzy about how old she was. They'd been married for several years, so no one was counting months any more. Not to mention that in those days people didn't think it was polite to pry.''

Florrie turned to me and said, "That's the curse of being a judge's wife. What use is a husband who knows all the really good gossip if he never tells you any of it? Anyway, lunch should be ready, so let's go eat while you tell him the rest of the story." And to him she said, "We have to figure out how to keep her out of jail, Hunter. She's practically family."

SO, OVER A delicious lunch in a beautifully appointed dining room, I told my story for the second time that day. I am proud to say that Molly did not disgrace me by begging for tidbits but seemed content to lie under the table with her new Rottie pals.

"And you say Tally doesn't know who Dolly was?" Hunter asked, as I wound up the story with the man who had come to question Madelyn.

"She didn't know who Dolores Miller was. I haven't asked her yet if she knows who Dolly Buchner was."

"It's probably time to give her a call." I gave him her number at FR&R and we all moved back to the living room.

After he got Tally on the phone and exchanged cousinly greetings, he said, "You'll never guess where your Lexy's inquiries have taken her." He listened for a moment and then said, "Not just at our front door, but sitting in our living room." He listened for another moment and then handed me the phone.

"Hey, Tally—I think I may be making some headway. Does the name Dolly Buchner mean anything to you?"

"Maybe. There was a Dolly that Susan used to occasionally take me to see years ago. I suppose it could have been Buchner. She lived down around San Jose or some place like that."

"Gilroy?" I asked.

"It certainly could have been Gilroy, but I was pretty young at the time and don't really remember. I guess she must have moved away because we stopped going to see her."

"She moved to Santa Barbara in the 'seventies. Was there a Mr. Buchner, do you know?"

"I think there was, although I don't remember him. Why? Is it important?"

"I don't know. But if there was a Mr. Buchner, she would've had another name before that. That's the trouble with trying to keep track of women; they just keep changing their names on you."

Florrie spoke up, saying, "There was a Mr. Buchner, and I think she married him in Gilroy. I always assumed she was a widow but I don't really recall. She didn't talk about herself much. I haven't any idea what her maiden name was."

I went back to the phone and asked, "Did you hear what Florrie said?"

"Yes. I don't know, either."

"Well, if I'm going to try to trace her back to Westchester, I'll need to know what her name was."

Florrie said, "I could try Madelyn again. She probably doesn't know, but Dolly may have had some papers that Madelyn would let me look at."

"As long as you take the girls with you. Madelyn's goldie doesn't look like much in the way of protection," I said.

"Don't worry; they'll be with me," Florrie answered.

"So Florrie still has her personal bodyguards," Tally said in my ear.

"Yup. Maybe we should get you some. After all, the killer is headed in your direction."

"You should talk, you with an attack Westie." Molly had a deserved reputation for not being much help in that respect, since she never barked at people. The best I could expect from her should we be intruded upon was that she'd untie the intruder's shoes, but she'd abandoned even this endearing, if annoying, puppy trick a few years back.

"I'VE MADE A FEW phone calls; I don't think you'll be going to jail," Hunter said a while later as he rejoined us in the living room, "but a certain detective in LA is a little unhappy and wants to talk to you very much. I told him to get in touch with you at the San Carlos."

"Detective Bruce Morita?" I asked.

"Yes. Is he the one you had your friend pump?"

"That's him."

"Well, I suggest you be a model of cooperation when you talk to him."

"I understand. And I'm very grateful to both of you."

"You needn't be—this is a family matter, and we're just as concerned as you are," Hunter replied, and Florrie nodded in agreement. "If we're finished here, I have to head back to the courthouse. Why don't you let me drop you off at the Santa Barbara Inn?"

I made my farewells to Florrie. Hunter and I chatted idly about dogs and Colorado while we covered the short distance to the Santa Barbara Inn. It wasn't until I was gathering myself and Molly to get out of the car that he spoke of my mission. "I'm glad Tally has you; if there's anything you need from me, I'm completely at your disposal."

Molly and I walked over to the beachfront. The most Molly had ever waded in before was the Boulder reservoir and I thought she ought to have a taste of the ocean. I also needed some time to think.

Dolly never talked about herself. Was she naturally reticent or was she hiding something? Had her coming to California been a coincidence, or was there some tie-in with Susan and Peter? Did she and Tally perhaps come with them? That would explain Hunter's remark that they had left New York without a baby and arrived in California with one. And did Dolly, or for that matter, Susan, actually know who Tally's birth parents were? Dolly had known about Tally all along—what prompted her to suddenly contact Tally in Los Angeles? Was the connection between Tally and her birth parents really what was driving this whole thing? Why had all these things that had apparently been dormant for so long suddenly come to life?

The sense that I had had earlier in the day that things were starting to move was obliterated by a new sense that I didn't really know anything and didn't know what string to pull next, either. In the absence of anything better to do, it was probably time to go face-to-face with the LA police and, with that prospect in mind, we retrieved the car and headed back to LA.

"I'd like," I said, "if you and Molly can you put Molly in that room?"
"Here. Call you." "Yeah. Yeah you're right. She wanted him by your side."
I shuddered, not wanting to think what I really might have gone lower. In the lot home of her life, I parked

SEVEN

As I SWEPT UP the long driveway of the San Carlos Court, an LAPD police cruiser fell in behind me, flashed its blue and whites at me briefly, and, once I had pulled into a parking space, parked across my rear end, blocking any hope of escape.

He was out of his car before I was out of mine and waiting by my door as I extricated myself and Molly. For a brief moment I regretted that I was wearing my dress sweats. What good was my power suit going to do me sitting in the closet in my room?

"Detective Morita, I presume," I said, extending my hand, which I was happy to see he merely shook in return, rather than cuffing it.

"Yes, Ms. Connor."

"If you'll just let me walk the dog a little, we can go inside and talk. I'm not going to run."

"You sure aren't," he replied and stuck close as I took Molly to the designated area.

And then, once again, and for the third time that day, I launched into my story. As I went on, he became less and less annoyed that I had tried to put something over on him and more and more interested in the details of the story.

"The man who questioned Mrs. Cross didn't come from us," he said. "I'll need a description of him. Santa Barbara PD should have told us about him."

"Tell me," I said, "if you find him, can you put him in that room?"

"Yes. Dolly put up a fairly good fight. She scratched him, for one thing."

I shuddered, not wanting to think what Dolly might have gone through in the last hours of her life. I picked up Molly and hugged her to ward off the evil.

"Listen," I said, "police interrogations always make me hungry and I'm starving. Would it violate your ethics to let me buy you a hamburger at Hamburger Hamlet while you finish your third degree?"

"This is an interview, Ms. Connor, not an interrogation. Trust me, you would be able to tell the difference." He actually laughed as he said that, and I relaxed considerably.

"Okay, police interviews always make me hungry. How about it?"

"You being pals with a district judge and all that, I think we'd better go dutch."

"Shame on you, Detective. Don't you know that 'going dutch' isn't politically correct?"

"Right, but the Dutch community in West Los Angeles has been pretty quiet on the subject lately, so we have the occasional lapse."

I, for one, was fairly happy to see that Detective Morita was known in the Hamburger Hamlet on San Vicente as, in the face of a large waiting crowd, the hostess greeted us with, "Hello, Detective Morita. You're right on time for your reservation," and showed us to a booth that was just being cleared.

"I'd forgotten what a busy place this is on weekends," I said. "I haven't been here in years." We chatted inconsequentially about the area, avoiding any touchy topics like celebrity murder trials.

Finally I said, "Okay. Tell me why you decided to tell Wes what you told him about Dolly Miller."

"Oh, that. It was a calculated risk. I was pretty sure he wasn't going to give me what he had voluntarily and I had already exhausted what little information we had, so I was hoping that setting him on the trail might shake something loose and, sure enough, it did. I suppose I could have taken him in the back room and sweated it out of him, but I figured there would be time enough for that later if I decided it was warranted. I've known him for a long time; he wouldn't have held out on me for long. And I have results only a day later. I mean, it isn't much, but it's more than I had. Knowing that there is a probable motive that explains the evidence will keep us from spinning our wheels on other possibilities. Besides, a judge now owes me a favor, so, all things considered, giving Wes the information I gave him paid off pretty well. But don't tell him that. Let him think he owes me one."

"Okay, it's a deal. But I owe *him* one, so don't be too tough on him."

Our burgers arrived and kept us occupied for a while. I find it a great tragedy that most Americans today have been raised on a diet of fast food hamburgers and have no idea how exquisite a burger can be when it is done right with quality ingredients. Many of the old LA coffee shops that had been driven out of business by the drive-through fast food chains turned out really delicious hamburgers, but the Hamburger Hamlets, a somewhat more upscale operation, were among the best.

"Wes says you always make him eat sushi," I said as I paused to wipe some grease off my chin.

"I only do that because he's always laying his West Texas country boy routine on me. It keeps things in balance.'' Poor Wes wouldn't be happy to know how transparent he was.

I spoke again after a few more mouthfuls, "I have a question about the autopsy.''

"What is it?''

"Did it indicate whether or not Dolores Miller had ever had a baby?''

"Yes, it did, and, no, she didn't. Were you thinking she might have been the birth mother?''

"It crossed my mind, but I didn't think it was very likely.''

"Why not?''

"Well, certainly Hunter and Flora Snowden would have noticed any likeness between her and Tally, for one thing. For another, I can't imagine her staying out of Tally's life like she did if she were the birth mother. And I think the birth mother's initials are 'PJ.' Would Dolly have put something in the note about 'PJ' if Dolly was the birth mother? I can't see it.''

"I'd like that note. You can bring it to me Monday when you come into the station to give your statement.''

"It's in Boulder. We didn't think it was too smart for me to be carrying it around.''

"Okay, you can fax it to me as soon as you get back to Boulder.''

"I'm not going back to Boulder," I said, "but I can have my housekeeper do it.''

"But there isn't anything more you can do here, is there?'' he asked.

"No, I'm not staying here, either.''

"I don't want you going to Gilroy. It's too danger-ous. We'll find out anything there is to find out in Gilroy faster than you will. I'll even be a sport and tell you what we find out.''

"That's great, I really appreciate it. But I wasn't going to go to Gilroy, either.''

"Then where are you going?''

"I'm going to hang around a day or so here to find out what you learn in Gilroy, and if there's no point in my going up there, I'm heading for Westchester.''

"I want you to go home and stay out of sight. It's not safe for you to go to Westchester.''

"With all due respect, Detective, you and I have some mutual interests here, but we don't have the same objectives. You need to solve a Los Angeles murder. I need to make sure that Tally is safe for all time. You're not going to do that and nobody else is, either. I'm the only one at the moment who can take that one on. I've got to find out who they are before they find out who she is, and I have no idea how close they might be.''

"It's too dangerous.''

"The only people who know my part in this aren't going to talk about it, so nobody knows who I am or what I'm after. I'm as safe as I can be, and if I blunder into something and get into trouble, I'll have only myself to blame.''

"I'll talk to the police back there for you.''

"Do me no favors. If my 'old cop' is in fact an old cop, he's most likely to be an old cop on some Westchester County police force. All we need to do is post an announcement that I'm coming and I'm useless, if not worse.''

Detective Morita was annoyed with me again, I could tell. I was grateful for the judge in my pocket. Evidently Morita resigned himself because at last he said, "We should have whatever we're going to get from Gilroy by early Tuesday.''

"Thank you," I replied.

"It comes with a price," he said.

"What's that?"

"That you give me any information you get and you keep me posted on what you're doing. That way, if you get yourself into trouble, at least the judge and I between us may be able to help you out."

"Deal," I said.

"How are you planning to go about identifying the birth mother?"

"I'm going to high school."

"What?"

"Susan's clue, the ring, points to a high school connection of some sort. I know the initials of the person I'm looking for, or at least some of them; I know she probably lived in that area; and I know all those high schools keep their old yearbooks in their libraries. I have to look in those old yearbooks."

"That'll be fun."

"Yeah, I think so, too."

EIGHT

THE PHONE RANG Sunday afternoon just as Molly and I were coming in from a stroll around Beverly Hills in the residential area between Wilshire and Sunset, west of Santa Monica Boulevard, in violation of the un-written law that no one walks in Beverly Hills.

"Lexy? It's Flora Snowden. I've just come back from Madelyn Cross's house and I thought you'd want to know what I discovered, or, rather, what I didn't discover."

"Didn't discover?"

"Didn't. Dolly Miller had a social security card is-sued in the name Dolores Buchner just before she came to work for me, a driver's license, her marriage license from her marriage to Dan Miller, Miller's death certif-icate, an annuity that ended at her death, a passbook for a largish savings account, a healthy checking ac-count, a hundred thousand dollar paid-up life insurance policy with Madelyn's kids as the beneficiaries, a one-page holographic will leaving everything else to Ma-delyn, the statutory seven years' worth of tax returns, and absolutely nothing else. Nothing. No address book, no credit cards, no letters, no Christmas cards, no pho-tos, no junior prom program, no high school graduation program, no newspaper clippings—no memorabilia of any type—no nothing. Madelyn says there isn't a safety deposit box, either, and the family lawyer doesn't have any personal papers other than a copy of the will and the deed to the house. There are some trusts that paid her and Madelyn a nice income, but they weren't in her name, they're in Madelyn's name."

"That's incredible. Did she live in the twentieth century?"

"That's what Hunter and I thought. We think the only reasonable conclusion is that she was already in hiding when she got to Gilroy and maybe Susan and Peter were the only ones who knew her real identity."

"It sure looks that way."

"One other thing. While I was at the house, Madelyn went out to run some errands and left me there with just the girls. Shortly after she left, someone came up on the porch and was fiddling with the door. The girls went absolutely berserk, which is what they're supposed to do, of course. By the time I got to the door and got them calmed down, a car was pulling away from the curb. I thought it just might be your old cop come back for another look at the house—maybe even looking for the same stuff I was looking for."

"You mean he was watching the house to see when Madelyn left and didn't know you were there?"

"Yes, I'd been there for quite a while, so he might not have seen me come in. Anyway, I don't think he'll be back in any big hurry."

"Hurray for the good guys. Too bad you didn't catch him, too."

"You said it. How'd you get along with the LA police?"

"All things considered, I did pretty well. Hunter has a lot of clout."

"Thank God for that. They're awfully touchy down there these days."

"With cause."

"I wouldn't argue with that."

"I will have to tell them about your would-be visitor today; they may be asking some questions. I know they want to talk to Madelyn and get a description."

"Oh, the Santa Barbara police already did that yesterday evening. Somebody lit a fire under somebody."

I SHOWED UP as scheduled on Monday to give my statement to Detective Morita. I told him about Florrie Snowden's phone call.

"The girls?" he said.

"Oh, didn't I tell you about Florrie's personal bodyguards? Four beautifully trained Rottweilers. She had the two females with her at Madelyn Cross's house yesterday."

He looked at me ruefully. "And you with one small terrier."

"That's what everybody says, but she's very sweet and almost beautifully trained."

He didn't respond to that, but flipped on his computer.

"Any new developments on your end?" I asked.

"No," he said, "but I hadn't expected anything to happen yet—small town police departments don't generally operate at full strength on weekends, so I imagine the Gilroy people didn't even look at our request until today. Okay, let's start at the top. First of all, I need your full name. Alexandra? Alexis?"

"Margaret Addison Connor."

"Margaret?"

"Yes, Margaret. Lexy is just a nickname I picked up about thirty years ago but I use it everywhere. All my legal papers list Lexy as an also known as."

"Okay, we can do that. It's kind of a strange nickname for someone called Margaret, though."

"I like the name Margaret well enough," I said, "but I can't stand any of the common nicknames for Margaret and the full three syllables just seem to be too much for many people."

"Where did the Lexy come from?" he asked.

"It's kind of involved."

"Involved is your middle name. Tell me."

"Okay. A long time ago in New York there was a coffee commercial on TV that was set in a South American mountain village. All of the peasants are very tense because the coffee buyer is coming to sample their coffee. He arrives, tries the coffee, and pronounces it good. A great fiesta breaks out because he has approved the coffee. The coffee buyer is referred to by all the peasants as El Exigente, because of his demand for excellence. Some people I worked with at the time started calling me El Exigente, which I considered very flattering—at least, I always assumed they meant it to be flattering. Anyway, it quickly got shortened to Lexy and then I just appropriated it."

The phone rang just then and Detective Morita answered it.

The conversation was one-sided, so I couldn't make anything out of the minimal responses at his end of it, but when he hung up, he looked at me and said, "Madelyn Cross's house was broken into this morning."

"Omigod, is she all right?"

"Yes, she and the children were out at the time. A neighbor saw someone in the house and, knowing there had been some problems with prowlers and that Mrs. Cross was out, she called the police, but he was gone by the time they got there. Santa Barbara is now very interested in this case. They don't like it when we, as he just put it, dump our big city messes on their doorstep. And, I might add, they don't like it when judges' wives are upset. Mrs. Cross and her children have gone to stay with the Snowdens until we get this cleared up, and apparently Mrs. Snowden has indicated that she expects that to be soon.''

"She's quite a woman," I answered. "You'd be impressed."

"Well, the Santa Barbara police certainly seem to be impressed."

"I'll bet. Did he succeed in searching the house this time?"

"It appears to have been thoroughly searched."

"So he found the same stuff Florrie Snowden found."

"No, he didn't even find that much—she took it all with her yesterday and gave it to the police today. He couldn't have found anything unless there was something she overlooked."

Just then another policeman came over and motioned Bruce away from the desk for a private conversation. Bruce returned just a moment later.

"We can finish this later. We need to go back to the San Carlos—we just got a call from a desk clerk who's been on vacation all week and didn't know until today about the death. He thinks he may have some information for us."

Gratified to be included, I gathered myself up and followed Bruce out to his car. I was happy to see that today we weren't driving around in a police cruiser, and decided that the one I had been treated to on Saturday had been intended to impress me. It had worked, in a manner of speaking, except that I had already decided to tell all.

The clerk was young, earnest, and gangly—all elbows and knees and jawbone and Adam's apple. The manager lent us his tiny office for the interview and excused himself.

To Bruce's questions the clerk answered that he was James Sanders, twenty-two years old, lived with his mother in West LA, had been on vacation since six o'clock Friday, August 30, until this morning, and had been in Mexico with friends and so had missed the news. And he may have seen the person who was with Dolores Miller when she died.

"She'd stopped to pick up her key—I'd checked her in over the telephone a couple of hours earlier; she said she needed to know her room number. Anyway, just as she was walking out of the lobby to her car, this guy comes up to me and grabs my arm and says, 'Who is that?' and points to her. 'Mrs. Miller,' I said. I thought he was going to check in, too, but instead he goes charging out after her. I never saw him again."

"What time was this?" Bruce asked.

"Around four-thirty, I guess. I left a little early myself so I could make my flight, and I usually leave at five."

"You think he was planning on checking in?"

"He'd been standing behind her waiting and I just assumed he was waiting to check in. When she turned around is when he thought he recognized her, I guess."

"Did you have any no-shows?"

"I hadn't thought of that. We can go look. They're kept in the system if they're guaranteed because we can still bill for them. But we get lots of walk-ins here, too, so he may not have had a reservation. Lots of people don't like to make guaranteed reservations because it can tie up their credit card limit and if they don't cancel, they still have to pay. And if he had a reservation and called and canceled before six o'clock, it would have been removed from the system anyway."

"Before we do that, can you describe him?"

"Well, he was an old guy, probably in his sixties. I really didn't get a good look at his face. He was maybe five-ten or so, about two hundred pounds, wearing a rumpled gray suit. He had gray hair and a sort of grayish complexion—he was kind of gray all over, if you know what I mean. And he was an easterner."

"An easterner? How could you tell?"

"He was wearing a hat. Nobody in LA wears that kind of hat."

"What kind of hat?" Bruce asked.

"A dress-up hat—you know, a straw one."

Bruce and I looked at each other.

"No one in the east wears that kind of hat in August, either, unless they're...I'm willing to bet he's bald," I said.

The hat was new news—he may have just gotten off a plane or something—but the description, such as it was, matched Madelyn's visitor.

A few minutes later, with the list of no-shows in hand, neither of the two entries very promising, we headed back to the police station.

The rest of my session with Detective Morita was uneventful. After I signed my statement, I headed back to the hotel to catch up on my communications chores.

I logged on to the Internet, read my mail, caught up with my newsgroups, and made flight, hotel, and car rental reservations for the next day. Then I called Tally to bring her up to date; Florrie and Madelyn to do the same; Debbie, to send ahead to Westchester some clothes more suitable to its climate in September; and

Wes, to tell him he was off the hook with Detective Morita.

Florrie and Madelyn had nothing new to offer, except that they were getting along famously, dogs and all. It occurred to me that maybe there was a new friendship blooming here that would compensate in some ways for the loss of Dolly.

Debbie was more than happy to send the clothes I wanted, but she was really reluctant to let Molly go on to New York. I finally had to put my foot down and say there was no way I was stopping in Colorado to leave Molly in her care. I think that Debbie, like most westerners, is suspicious of anything having to do with New York and feared its possibly corrupting influence on Molly. I didn't tell her that Molly had already succumbed to the inducements of life in the big city, including room service and minibars.

Wes decided that his not being hauled off to jail for withholding evidence was reason for celebration and that we should have dinner, which struck me as a highly agreeable plan. He then went on to improve on that by insisting that he would take us to the airport the next day, so I wouldn't have to cope with returning the rental car along with getting myself and Molly on the plane, so I turned in my car before we went to dinner.

Wes understands completely the principle of "love me, love my dog," so he took us to dinner at his club, where we could dine on the terrace with Molly in attendance. I figured once she knew about room service, there was no point in any longer trying to keep the secret of restaurants from her. At least we weren't in France, so she wouldn't expect a place to be set at the table for her. Anyway, she seemed to understand that perfect manners were expected of her under the circumstances and she once more made me proud, although I was also grateful that no cats chose that occasion to stroll across the terrace.

We laughed together all evening long as only old friends can who have no need to conceal their frailties or failures or to be modest about their successes.

DETECTIVE MORITA called me early on Tuesday to fill me in on the situation in Gilroy. Our man had been there on Friday, but could not have learned very much because there was nothing much to learn. Dolly had arrived in town in 1966 or 1967 using the name "Dolores Morgan," but there was no evidence that there had ever been a Dolores Morgan before that day. She had worked as a live-in housekeeper until she married Carl Buchner in 1969. The family she worked for originally had left for parts unknown by the end of the 'sixties.

Everybody thought the Buchner marriage was a happy one. Buchner had died in the late 'seventies of pancreatic cancer, leaving Dolly a modest but comfortable inheritance. Buchner was remembered fairly well, but few people seemed to know Dolly, and apparently when she left to go to Santa Barbara, no one seemed to notice or care.

I interrupted him, saying, "That doesn't seem consistent with how well liked she was in Santa Barbara."

"I think she was still keeping a very low profile in Gilroy; by the time she got to Santa Barbara, she may have felt safer."

We ended our conversation with his again warning me to be careful and to keep him posted.

Wes arrived as scheduled to take us to the airport, which simplified the whole process. With the inducement of a little piece of Brie, Molly went into her travel cage with hardly a murmur, and we were off again.

NINE

LIVING IN COLORADO, it is possible to forget just how long a coast-to-coast flight can be. Despite snoozing, I was exhausted when we landed at La Guardia that evening and wasn't looking forward to the task of recovering my dog and my luggage and wrestling all of it to where I could pick up the Hertz bus. I have a dim memory that there were once skycaps at La Guardia, but I couldn't remember in what era I had last seen one. Thus it was with great pleasure that I saw my niece Sheila waiting at the gate. Such are the unexpected pleasures resulting from e-mail; I had sent her a note yesterday telling her of my plans to be in the area, adding that she would finally have an opportunity to meet Molly.

"Oh, you have no idea how glad I am to see you," I said when I got close enough for her to hear me.

"You'll be even gladder when you see what I brought you," she answered, producing from behind her back a pooper scooper. "You'll need this in New York."

After I had exclaimed appropriately over the thoughtfulness of that gift, she produced another from the other hand—a bag marked "Wolf's Delicatessen," which I knew would contain corned-beef-and-pastrami sandwiches on Kaiser rolls with cole slaw and Russian dressing.

"I figured you wouldn't have time to get a decent dinner."

"Well, not time enough to get one *that* good," I answered. "You're a godsend."

"I thought you could probably use a hand at this end, and I knew that you'd want some good food after an airline dinner."

She was right on both counts. After we retrieved Molly we sat down on a bench and had our sandwiches—she had even brought a plain cheeseburger for Molly—and watched the traffic pick its way through the latest construction at La Guardia. When I was younger, I preferred the more glamorous accommodations at JFK, but these days I appreciate the greater convenience of La Guardia even more. I think JFK lost its charm for me when TWA started routing domestic arrivals and departures through a new and very ordinary terminal, leaving their original building to international flights. I know now that I flew TWA for years primarily for the thrill of walking through that incredible Eero Saarinen building with its soaring interior spaces.

Of course now, living as I do in Colorado, United is virtually the only choice; the other majors have token flights to Denver from their hubs, but United owns the local traffic, lock, stock, and barrel.

The downside of using La Guardia is that it is forever in an advanced state of chaos from constant construction that can never keep up with New Yorkers' insatiable demand for more transportation capacity. Whatever an architect may have intended as effect is completely lost in the maze of temporary roadways, construction fences, and turmoil of an overworked facility.

Our inner persons having been excellently dealt with, I left Sheila to entertain Molly while I got the car. When I finally made my way back to them, Molly was resting on the bench with her head on Sheila's thigh.

"Isn't it amazing what one cheeseburger will buy you?" I asked.

"One cheeseburger and a lot of head rubbing," she answered as we stowed everything in the car, a mere Taurus this time.

Sheila insisted it was not necessary for me to drive her home before I headed north, but I love Manhattan and wanted to reconnect with what I remembered from my twenties. On such a journey, though, it's best to move quickly because if you linger, you discover that nothing is actually the same, and you lose a little bit of your sense of knowing this place.

Sheila lived in Alphabet City, a part of Manhattan that is alien to me. I had lived on the Upper East Side and worked in midtown, with occasional forays into the Village, but in all those years I was never quite certain where Alphabet City could be found, except that it was vaguely east of the East Village. Sheila would let me pick her up and drop her off there, but she wouldn't let me actually get out of the car. She didn't think I was tough enough, and I thought she was probably right. As a matter of simple fact, I didn't think she was tough enough, either, but my opinion on the matter wasn't wanted and at least it was the devil she knew.

As we made our way into Manhattan, she quizzed me about why I had come and I filled her in. Sheila had lived with me for several months while I was the Richards' tenant, so she and Tally, almost the same age, had become friends, if not bosom buddies.

"What's a friendship ring?" she asked.

"Just an ordinary ring with an inexpensive gemstone; it was a brief fad for girls to give them to each other as birthday presents when I was in high school. You'd have them engraved with the recipient's initials. If you didn't have any friends, you could always buy your own.''

I dropped her off in Alphabet City and found my way to Third Avenue, which usually gives you a pretty clear shot uptown later in the evening. Molly was clearly not thrilling to the beat of this incredible city, but snoozing again. Still, hers was a companionable presence as we left the lights of Manhattan behind and headed into the darker reaches of the Bronx and Westchester.

I KNOW PEOPLE who respond viscerally to the vast flat sweeps of the prairie, and those who love the rolling hills of Virginia, and those for whom the craggy peaks of the Rockies sing out, and those for whom there is nothing that can surpass California's golden hills and mist-shrouded coast, but for me it is the lush greenery of the northeast corridor that has a siren call.

In the springtime, when the azaleas and rhododendrons are in bloom, there are parts of Westchester County that could make you weep for their splendor. The rest of the year, as now, they are merely beautiful. Deep summer makes everything—trees, lawns, and shrubs—an intense dark green, and the white Colonial Revival houses and their neighboring dark Tudors look like antique jewels in a green setting.

The gracious homes set in wide green lawns speak of a serene age now long gone. The county is presently headquarters for many of America's corporate giants, but that influx didn't begin until the 'sixties. The areas flanking the Hutchinson River Parkway and running from there east to the mainland shore of Long Island Sound had been the venue of wealth and privilege to rival any in the country for better than half a century before that.

Westchester has had its celebrity murders, too—the diet doctor and his headmistress lover come to mind— but Westchesterites would rather go sailing than go and gawk at scenes of moral collapse among the rich and famous.

I had settled myself at the Hutchinson River Heights Inn. It probably should be noted that the Hutchinson River has no heights that anyone has ever taken note of, and that the hotel would be more aptly named the Hutchinson River Parkway Blasted Bluffs Inn, since some of its natural setting was likely the result of blasting away a hillside to make way for the parkway, but it was a more than adequately comfortable establishment in a woodland setting. Better than that, it had a cheerful tolerance for canine guests and first floor rooms with private, walled patios. No having to get dressed at seven in the morning to take the dog out!

The color scheme this time was teal and taupe, a post mauve-and-celadon period, I conjectured. Again, there was the pair of color-keyed paintings over the bed. I had visions of hotel-painting artists being locked in a room stocked with tubes of only teal and taupe (or mauve and celadon, depending on the period) acrylics and acres of blank canvases.

It was dark when I arrived, so I took some time in the morning to absorb the beauty of the forest beyond my patio, at the same time taking steps to reassure Molly that the room service here would meet her standards.

It had also occurred to me that I needed a plan of attack. Of all the high schools in Westchester, I knew the whereabouts of only two of them, including my own. I decided it was time for a little subterfuge and chicanery, so I pulled out the yellow pages and found the address of a real estate office affiliated with the real estate company whose telemarketing techniques I had found the most objectionable over the years. Payback time!

By mid-morning, I found the office in one of those little frame cottages set back from the Boston Post Road, hitched Molly on my hip and walked in, mentally reviewing my cover story.

I was greeted by a middle-aged woman wearing a too-bright blazer with the company logo on the breast pocket, too much makeup, and a plastic smile.

"Good morning," I said, insinuating myself into the chair across from her desk without waiting for an invitation. "I was referred to this office by a friend of mine," I gushed. "She said you'd taken good care of her."

"Well, isn't that nice," she gushed back. "How can we help you?"

"I'm looking for some information about schools. My daughter is moving to this area from Short Hills in a few months and I'm doing some advance scouting for her two high school-age daughters." I knew that the reference to Short Hills would get her attention, and just hoped she wouldn't expect me to know anything about Short Hills, where I had never been.

"We have very fine schools here in Westchester. You can hardly go wrong around here, either public or private."

I choked a little on that. I hadn't even considered the possibility of a private school. They might be a little less accessible for my purposes. My instinct was to start with the public schools in any case; I had to start somewhere and I wasn't sure I knew how to go about it with the public schools, let alone the private ones. "Oh, I'm sure all the schools are excellent, but I promised my granddaughters that I would actually go to the schools and check out their facilities and their programs. Their parents would be here themselves but they are too busy and the girls are, of course, in school. I'll start with the public schools; the girls weren't too happy with the notion of private schools and here, of course, one expects to be able to find public schools with excellent academic and social standards. But, please, I don't want to take up too much of your time," I trailed off, thinking: *Tell me what I want to know and I'm out of here like a shot.*

Like the answer to a prayer, she produced a school district map of the county. She gripped it tightly while she discussed the relative merits of the various schools and I contemplated grabbing it from her hand and making a dash for the door. Instead, I smiled and nodded and said a lot of "Uh-huhs" and "I sees" and "Hmms" until she started to wind down.

Finally, I said, "I really don't want to take up any more of your time until they've settled on which area they're definitely interested in," baiting the trap with a promise to return with a real house-buyer in tow. "Might I have a copy of that map?" She'd pulled it from a stack, so I knew it was expendable, but I didn't know if I had yet convinced her that this was a bird in the hand and worth giving up her treasure.

Reluctantly, she handed it over. Not that it mattered, but I hoped I hadn't blown my cover in my eagerness to be out the door, prize in hand—I was on my way to the street in only seconds, so I couldn't be sure. In any case, I knew I had struck one tiny blow for telemarketing haters everywhere.

I turned east from the Boston Post Road and drove sort of aimlessly, keeping as close as I could to the water, until I found a little park looking out on Larchmont Harbor where I could sit on a bench and let Molly explore while I planned my attack. I hadn't realized how difficult this could be, given the distraction offered by the view. For a while I watched the launches running back and forth between the club docks and the clusters of sailboats riding at anchor in the harbor and reminisced about long ago summers and flirtations with launch boys. I was never one of the sailing set but a number of my friends were, so I had seen the inside of more than one yacht club on the sound, although none so fancy as the one I was looking at now. Were I a sailor, this would seem to be the perfect day for sailing, and it wasn't hard to imagine what attracted people to it in a setting like this.

I finally forced my attention back to the map by reminding myself that I was on the clock and that some very unfriendly people were threatening unfriendly things. Of course, we had identified only one villain so far, and we hadn't really identified him, but I was fairly certain that, in the long run, we would have more than one such to deal with.

Susan had gone to Kingsbridge High, so that was an obvious place to begin, but if Dolly Miller was the actual link, then Susan may not have known PJ at all and even the assumption that PJ had gone to school in the same county was suspect. I pushed that thought from my mind because I had no idea how to proceed if I didn't go ahead with the local high schools. After all, the ring must have been intended to communicate something. With Larchmont as the center, I started listing schools in ever-widening circles, counting myself lucky that Larchmont backed up against Long Island Sound and there weren't any high schools to be found in Long Island Sound.

It was time to go to work. I dropped Molly back at the hotel, introducing her to the day staff, who assured me that they would look out for her and that she could safely stay on the patio. I also called Florrie Snowden to ask her to back me up on my cover story, should the need arise.

Then I headed back to Kingsbridge High.

Kingsbridge, like many of the high schools in Westchester, had been built in a time when architectural distinction was an objective. It had a distinctly Gothic look, unlike modern schools, which resemble nothing so much as bunkers. I took a deep breath and my first step inside a high school in nearly forty years.

High schools are an alien environment to me, but then I have to remind myself that they were an alien environment back in my student days as well. It wasn't until I was much older that I came to understand that alienation was a normal state for a teenager. I wish someone had told us that when were going through it. It might have made things a little easier, but probably not.

Looking at the Kingsbridge students, I felt a sense of gratitude that my high school days had occurred in the era of the preppie look, and we went about in crew-neck sweaters, button-down shirts, plaid skirts, knee socks, and penny loafers. When it comes to teen fashion, I must confess to being the fuddiest of old duddies.

I came into the administration office during a class period, so things were relatively quiet, and approached a harried-looking clerk.

"I wonder if I might speak to someone about doing a small piece of research in your library?"

"There's a public library," she responded without much grace.

"Oh, I realize that," I said, "but I was particularly interested in looking at your yearbooks from the late 'fifties and early 'sixties." I leaned forward over the chest-high counter and dropped my voice to a whisper. "It's confidential research for a profile piece in the *New Yorker*," I said. "The party is quite famous today, or rather, she will be when she gets the prize, but no one seems to be aware that she went to high school here or how critical that experience was."

She apparently decided that, while this was not her decision to make, I was not a major security risk, because she said, "You'll have to ask the librarian for permission." She turned around to a student working at a desk behind her and said, "Tiffany, will you please show Ms.—" she swung back to me with a questioning expression on her face.

"Connor, Margaret Connor."

"Ms. Connor to the library and introduce her to Ms. Somers?"

Tiffany, apparently eager for a variation in the routine, acquiesced with a gracious smile and I was on my way. She was my first real live Tiffany and looked every inch the part. I would have liked to engage her in conversation about what it was like to be a Tiffany, but this seemed to be neither the time nor the place. Besides, I had to save all my energy for the climb to the second floor.

Ms. Somers was a young and very librarian-looking librarian, wearing the same navy blue gabardine skirt and white blouse uniform that had been worn by the librarian in my high school forty years earlier, except the blouse was now polyester instead of nylon. She practically swooned over the allusion to the *New Yorker* and couldn't do enough for me, pulling out a chair and patting the seat for me to sit down before she went charging off to retrieve the yearbooks I wanted. She was clearly dying to ask me questions and I assured her that when the profile was published, she would find herself appropriately credited, but for now it was necessary to be quite hush-hush. I was a little surprised at how easily I could lie like this; I suppose the practice round in the real estate agency made it easier.

Susan had graduated in 1960, so to cover all the people who might have been in the school at the same time she had, I was going to have to look at yearbooks from 'fifty-eight through 'sixty-two—these had all been three-year high schools at the time. I hadn't kept up with secondary education enough to know what they might be today.

When I got to 1960, I looked up Susan Franklin.

"Just look what you've gotten me into," I muttered to her teenaged face with its serene smile, and grabbed a hanky from my purse before I alarmed Ms. Somers with an un-*New-Yorker*ly display of emotion.

Then I went back to my task of looking for any possible candidate to be "PJ."

Kingsbridge High School yielded two candidates in those five years, neither of whom excited me very much as prospective mothers for Tally. I suppose it was expecting a little much to think that their list of high school accomplishments and future plans would include having a daughter, possibly outside of wedlock, and giving her up for adoption under mysterious circumstances.

I checked the names I found against the school's alumni directory, but neither of them were there. Westchester had been swept in the last few years by a firm whose business was alumni directories. I had been canvassed twice, once for my college directory and once for my high school one. Their success in locating alumni was somewhat better for the college directory—private colleges had a greater interest in tracking their alums than public high schools did.

TEN

BUCK TEETH (orthodontia wasn't covered by company health benefits in those days, so the straightening of crooked teeth that is virtually automatic among pre-teens today didn't happen then), receding chins, cardigan sweaters worn front to back (a style that escaped me then and still does), duck tails, Peter Pan collars—an endless display of high school fashion from the late 'fifties to the early 'sixties. I had to keep reminding myself of what I was searching for, and on more than one occasion had to retrace my steps when I realized that I'd been turning pages without actually seeing the names listed on them. I couldn't trust that the initials "PJ" were necessarily a first and last initial, so I had to find all of the names of girls with the first initial P. "Patricia" was the best-seller in those days, with an occasional "Priscilla" or "Phyllis" but happily "P" wasn't as popular a name-starter as I'd feared.

The dust from books that hadn't been looked at in decades invaded my sinuses and made my eyes burn and the hours of sitting in hopelessly uncomfortable library chairs did a number on my back. I was developing a deep sense of my own martyrdom, along with a conviction that this was a wild goose chase.

Two days and eight high schools, eight Tiffanies, and eight Ms. Somerses later, including two calls to Florrie, who was posing as a *New Yorker* editor, to check my cover story, I had a list of fifteen names, two of them with nearly current listings in high school alumni directories. I had also reached the end of the

school week, so there were no more libraries to plumb
for the time being.

I HAD FORGOTTEN how much traffic Westchester
County could generate for the Friday evening rush—
too much for its antiquated roads to handle. As I inched
along in the thick of Westchester Avenue traffic, I was
reminded of that Friday afternoon long past when I'd
witnessed a then-unusual crush of traffic backed up behind the Tappan Zee Bridge toll plaza, headed for
points northwest. Fortunately, I was going in the opposite direction. It wasn't until much later that I realized what I'd witnessed was traffic bound for Wood-
stock and the rock festival that, some would say,
changed the nation, if not the world. Today there was
no such common destination—just weary office workers headed for home and a gin and tonic before dinner
and New York City yuppies bound for a weekend in
the country.

It served to remind me of why I loved living in my
quiet little corner of Colorado, which, like every place
else, was becoming less quiet with each passing decade. Boulderites complained about the increase in traffic but, on its worst day, it still took only ten minutes
to get from any place in town to any other.

As I inched through the clogged streets, I amused
myself with thoughts of high school yearbook technology. I recalled reading recently that some high school
classes were putting their yearbooks on video tape. I
wondered if any of them realized how unsatisfactory a
tape would be after the first viewing. Of course, I consider tape an unsatisfactory medium for anything other
than movies, and not even those if reasonable life ex-

pectancy is a criterion. But I was probably already behind the times for almost certainly some high school media-mogul-to-be was already producing the yearbook in interactive CD form, if not putting it on the web.

Back in the hotel with Molly walked and now snuggled in my lap, I contemplated my list at length. I also had copies of the yearbook pages with their pictures on them, but the poor quality of the photos in the yearbooks compounded by the loss of quality from copying the pages on poorly maintained school library copiers meant the pictures didn't show me much. There were a few of them that looked more promising than others because of a faint resemblance to Tally, but for the most part the pictures were as distinctive as features painted on balloons. In any case, none of the pictures spoke to me and said, ''Me. I'm the one you're looking for.''

I created a spreadsheet on my laptop and loaded in the meager information I had about my fifteen candidates. This at least gave me the illusion that I was accomplishing something.

I've been in the computing industry long enough to remember when the popular press referred to them as ''giant electronic brains,'' but that evening my giant electronic brain just sat there and stared back at me, not offering any giant electronic brainwork at all.

I was not optimistic about the possibility of finding any of the people on my list, let alone all of them, or the right one. I considered the dispersion of my own high school acquaintances; I could only think of two of the handful whose whereabouts I knew at all that currently lived in Westchester County. The parents of my generation of Westchesterites had, for the most part, not been native to Westchester, and it was not a place that many of us had returned to to raise our own families, either. Personally, I found it a much more congenial environment now than I had when I was in my early twenties and lusted for a life in a slightly faster lane, but I didn't know many people who could afford it now.

So not only was there reason to doubt that my fifteen were living in Westchester County, there was also reason to doubt that they now used the same names as I had on the list in front of me. Statistically, I would expect roughly eleven or twelve of them to have married at least once, and they were of a generation that would routinely assume their husband's name. Of course, some of them might be divorced and have resumed their birth names. I might get lucky on one or two.

Not to mention what I thought I was going to do if I did manage to find any of them. "Pardon me for asking what might be considered a fairly personal question, but did you happen to have a baby girl in nineteen sixty-six that you gave up for adoption?"

When I didn't want to think about those things for a while, I thought about the likelihood that the person I was seeking wasn't even on my list. Maybe I hadn't gotten to the right high school, or maybe the ring wasn't meant to steer me to Westchester high schools at all. For a while, I considered the possibility of just continuing to canvass high schools in an ever-widening circle until I collapsed of library dust inhalation in the far reaches of New Hampshire. That idea had even less appeal than asking strangers about babies they might have had thirty years ago.

In this delightful frame of mind, I called Tally.

"This is a long shot," I said, after I had brought her up to date, which didn't take long, "but let me read the list to you to see if any of the names are familiar. I know this is stupid, but it would be even stupider if I never asked you and it turned out that one of them had been your babysitter all through your childhood."

"Read on," she said, and I read the list slowly and carefully, pausing for her response after each name.

"Sorry," she said, as we hit the last name, "not a babysitter in the lot. I've gone through Susan's papers, too, looking for any mention of a 'PJ,' and drew a blank."

"Maybe this would all be simpler if we just got you a pair of Rottweilers instead."

"Don't think Florrie hasn't suggested it," she said. "Speaking of Florrie, maybe you ought to call Santa Barbara and read the list to them; after all, they spent a lot of time with Dolly and Dolly might have talked about PJ at some point or another."

So my next call was to Santa Barbara. I laughed when Madelyn answered the phone, using the snooty accent and precise elocution that Florrie had taught her, "The *New Yorker*. How may I direct your call?"

"You don't have to do that any longer, at least not for the time being," I said.

"Shoot," she said. "We were kind of enjoying it. Let me get Florrie for you."

When Florrie came on the line, I said, "You were great; I had them eating out of my hand after they talked to you."

"It was the most fun I've had in a long time. It's going to be hard to give up the part—it's the only career I've ever had outside of being a judge's wife.

Have you made any progress? Madelyn tells me we're out of business here.''

"No more high schools for me, at least for now. I've got fifteen names to work on and that should keep me busy," I said.

I read the list to each of them in turn, with the same result as I had with Tally. I finished up with Hunter, who said, "I have someone you can call if you need any help or just need someone to talk to about this. He's an old friend of mine, a judge who just retired from the county bench back there, and he is a valuable contact for you to have in case you run into any problems." Hunter didn't say what kind of problems he expected me to run into, and I didn't ask. "His name is Charlie Seabrook," he said, giving me the number. "He's expecting to hear from you if you need him."

Short of calling him up and reading him the list of names, I couldn't think of any way he could be helpful at that juncture, so I just scribbled his name and number on the hotel message pad.

After a quick pizza in a local Italian eatery, I set to work on my list.

My first thought was that the two names from Kingsbridge High School were the most promising, simply because they had been in school with Susan. I fired up my phone listing software and entered "Hampden, Priscilla" within New York State. To my pleasant surprise, it came back almost immediately with a listing for "Hampden, Priscilla J" and a Croton address. Flushed with success, I tried the various possibilities for Patricia Cooley Jackson. I groaned when I saw the result. Taking together all of the "Jackson, P" entries, the "Jackson, P C" entries, the "Jackson, Patricia" entries, and the sole "Jackson, Patricia C" entry, there were over five hundred candidate listings in the tri-state area of New York, New Jersey, and Connecticut. Considering that there was also a Johnson, not to mention a Jones, on my list, I quickly narrowed the search to the local area codes and got a more manageable number of entries for each of those names. I continued the phone searches on the rest of the names except for the two for which I had alumni directory listings, and turned up some possible listings for the other names.

At the end of that session, I had my two alumni directory listings, a promising-looking phone listing, a very long list of people to call and ask if they by any chance graduated from such-and-such a high school in such-and-such a year, and a severe case of eyestrain. I called it a day.

ELEVEN

I HAVE AN aversion to calling (and being called by) strangers on the telephone, so I decided to postpone that activity as long as possible by going after the three PJs—Hampden, Farber, and Morris—whose addresses I knew. I conjectured, rightly or wrongly, that approaching them in person was likely to be more productive than approaching them on the phone, especially given the weirdness of my errand. I put Hampden first on my list because she was also the Kingsbridgian. It was too hot a day to leave Molly in the car, so alone I headed west, toward the Hudson River.

CROTON-ON-HUDSON. I didn't know it at all except for the platform in its railroad station. For some reason that now escapes me, but undoubtedly having to do with expresses and locals, the New York Central required one to change at Croton for some points north and to reverse the process on the way home. I surely must have made some of those trips in summer daylight, but in my memory it was always bitter cold and spookily dark on that platform.

My destination proved to be a 'sixties split-level of a spectacular ordinariness. A woman in jeans and a sweatshirt and a falling-apart ponytail was deadheading the rose bushes around the front door. She paused to watch me as I pulled up and got out of the car. When I got close enough, I could see that she was of a suitable age to be my quarry. She wiped a lock of hair out of her eyes with the back of her gloved hand and waited for me to speak.

"I'm looking for Priscilla Hampden," I said.

"You've found her," she answered.

"Are you the Priscilla Jane Hampden who graduated from Kingsbridge High School in Larchmont in nineteen fifty-eight?" I asked.

She said, "Who wants to know? And why?" She clearly wasn't feeling any need to be friendly, a sentiment to which I was entirely sympathetic, or would have been under other circumstances.

"My name is Lexy Connor, which shouldn't mean anything to you. I have recently come into possession of a piece of jewelry, a ring, that belongs to a woman with the initials 'PJ' and I'd like to return it to its owner. There's a possibility that you could be that owner."

"I haven't lost any jewelry," she answered.

"This would have been quite a while ago, not recently," I said.

"Not a while ago, either, that I can think of. How long ago?"

"In nineteen sixty-six or thereabouts."

"In nineteen sixty-six?" she said with a short, humorless laugh. "I didn't have any jewelry to lose in nineteen sixty-six. I hardly have any now. Besides, if I had, I'd have lost it in Guatemala. Did you find it in Guatemala, by any chance?"

"I'm not sure where it was lost; I think it may have traveled quite a bit before it came to me, so Guatemala isn't out of the question." While Guatemala wasn't out of the question, it certainly didn't fit in with anything else I thought I knew. "How long were you in Guatemala?"

"Two years, 'sixty-five and 'sixty-six. The Peace Corps. After I got my master's, I decided to go off and make the world a better place. I wanted Africa, but I got Guatemala. I came home with a much different attitude about saving the world and a tropical parasite in my large intestine. I spent the better part of 'sixty-seven in the can." I recognized this as a speech that had been used many times. "What's your interest in all this, anyway?" she asked.

"I think the woman who lost the ring would be very happy to be reunited with it."

"Well, it's not mine."

I was inclined to agree with her on that. The PJ I was looking for would certainly know the significance of the ring, and I couldn't detect any sign that Priscilla Hampden had reacted to the news of it at all. I couldn't eliminate her altogether based on this conversation, but she no longer headed my list.

"Could I ask you one more question?" I said.

"Sure, as long as you don't necessarily expect an answer."

"Did you by any chance know a girl by the name of Susan Franklin at Kingsbridge High?"

She gave me an odd look, as if she found this question even stranger than my other ones. "I knew who she was, but I can't say that I really knew her. What does this have to do with her?"

I shrugged and said, "If you're not the owner of the ring, I'm afraid I can't tell you what it is has to do with her. I appreciate your answering my questions and I'm sorry to have bothered you. If you think of anything you might want to tell me, you can call me at this number for at least the next few days." I handed her my card, on which I had written the number of the hotel.

When I turned the car around to head back the way I came, I saw she was back to deadheading the roses. Somehow I didn't think that my PJ would simply go back to deadheading her roses after that conversation.

PAMELA JACQUELINE Morris Stuart was listed in the Rose Hill High School alumni directory as living in Tenafly, New Jersey. I drove south from Croton through Ossining, Sleepy Hollow, and Tarrytown, all rich in colonial history, to the Tappan Zee Bridge, which had been built across one of the widest parts of the Hudson—a bridge placed a few miles to either side could have been much shorter. But, for whatever reason, this one was where it was, and its length afforded a leisurely enjoyment of its spectacular view of the river, looking both to the north and to the south, where the Manhattan skyline sat on the horizon.

A magnificent mansion had once stood in the bridge's path on the Tarrytown side. I remembered as a teen going on a photography expedition with my parents and finding this house, standing in a field of mud where its lawns had once been, with its doors wide open. We explored it from top to bottom, undisturbed by anyone telling us we shouldn't be there. There were still traces of its former life in the woodwork that hadn't yet been ripped from the walls, the pipes that were all that remained of an organ in the elliptical music room, and the primitive system used to summon servants from the kitchen quarters to the rest of the house. At that time the house had escaped any serious vandalism and it was easy to imagine that, with a little effort, it could be fixed up and put back into service. It had been painful to think that it would soon be gone.

It was quite possibly one of the more minor of the fabled Hudson River mansions, but it was the most splendid thing that I'd seen in my young life.

When we went past the spot a few months later, there was a deep cut in the raw earth where the house had stood.

I zipped over the bridge and headed south on the Jersey side of the Hudson to Tenafly, one of the many bedroom communities that line the top of the Palisades, this one due west from Yonkers.

The house was a modest 'fifties "ranchette," similar to its neighbors except for shallow ramps added to the step up to the walkway from the driveway and from the walkway to the porch, presumably to accommodate a wheelchair. I idly wondered if the wheelchair was Pamela Jacqueline's.

No one answered the doorbell. I stood irresolute on the tiny porch for a few minutes, when I suddenly realized that I hadn't eaten all day and I was hungry. I went back to the car and found my way into the main part of town, where I found something to eat and a bookstore. I had exhausted my supply of reading material in the hotel and had nothing with me to sustain me while waiting for someone to come home at the Stuart household. I restocked myself with mysteries and went back to the little house. I checked to see if anyone had returned in my absence, and when that got no result, I settled myself in the car to wait.

I am not the world's most patient person and I don't wait well. After two hours, and at an hour when most of the neighbors seemed to have returned home from wherever they had been for the day, I gave up and headed back to Westchester County, where I would be just in time to pick up Molly and go meet some old friends for dinner.

PEARL JOYCE Farber Branscomb was listed in her alumni directory as living in a Connecticut town whose name I didn't recognize, but my street atlas software showed the address as being about halfway between Bridgeport and New Haven, somewhere between the Merritt Parkway and the old Boston Post Road. The Hutchinson River Parkway becomes the Merritt when it crosses the border into Connecticut. A long drive to gamble that she'd be at home, but I liked driving the Merritt through Connecticut, so I went anyway.

This PJ had done rather better than her contemporaries in Croton and Tenafly, if the scale of one's house was any indicator. It was large, fairly new, and its setting by a small pond was nothing short of idyllic.

"I'm looking for Pearl Branscomb," I said to the petite and attractive woman who answered the door.

In return, my classic blazer and slacks got a careful scrutiny. Finally, she said, "Joyce Branscomb. I don't use 'Pearl'—in fact I didn't think anybody even knew it any more. Who told you that was my name?"

"Your high school alumni directory, as a matter of fact."

"Do you mean to tell me that I'm going to regret letting myself be listed in there?"

"I certainly hope not, or at least not on account of me. I'm not here to sell you anything, if that's what you mean."

"Then why are you here? Did I go to high school with you?"

"No, I went to a different school, and it's not high school that I'm here about. My name is Lexy Connor and I've come into possession of a piece of jewelry, a ring, that I think may possibly belong to you."

She glanced briefly at her elegantly manicured hands, which sported several rings that, if they were the real thing, were very impressive indeed.

"I'd have to check, but I don't think any of my rings are missing," she said.

"This wouldn't be one that you lost recently. I believe it was lost a long time ago."

"Let me see it, then," she said.

"I don't have it with me."

"Well, I don't know how I can tell whether it's mine or not without looking at it. Where did you find it?"

"It was given to me by a friend, but the friend has died and I'm trying to get the ring back to its owner."

"Look, if it's from the burglary, that was paid off by the insurance company, so I'm not interested. There's no reward, either, unless you take it to the insurance company. They may want to recover some of their losses."

She started to close the door on me. This wasn't going well at all.

"No, it's not from any burglary. It was lost a long time ago, probably in the mid-'sixties. Nineteen sixty-six."

She shook her head. "Nineteen sixty-six? I was in New York City then. That was when I was doing *The Fantasticks* Village. I understudied the lead and had a small part. Before Josh and I were married. In fact, that's how we met—he saw me in the show. He came several times a week for months before he got up the nerve to ask for a date. We were married in the spring of 'sixty-seven." Telling me this made her smile; she was still taken with the romance of it all. "But I don't remember losing any ring," she concluded.

"It has a blue stone, probably an aquamarine, and the initials 'PJ' inside."

She shook her head. "Not mine. I told you, I don't use my first name at all and never have."

"I guess I need to keep looking. Thank you for talking to me," I said, starting to turn away, when I had another thought. She had the door almost closed again, but opened it a little wider when I turned back toward it. "One more thing, if you don't mind. Do you by any chance know the whereabouts of a high school classmate of yours, Patricia Johnson?"

"Another 'PJ'?" she said, and I nodded in response. "We were in high school before nineteen sixty-six."

"I know, but the ring was probably a high school friendship ring from a few years earlier. It just wasn't lost until nineteen sixty-six."

"This is very curious."

"I know, but I can't really explain it until I find the right PJ," I said.

"As a matter of fact, I do know where Pat is; I ran into her only a couple of months ago at a fund-raiser and she gave me her number. But I'm not sure I should tell you."

"I'm only going to ask her the same question I asked you, but perhaps you'd rather call her first and get her permission, or have her call me."

She shrugged a little. "No. Do you mind waiting here while I get it?"

"Not at all," I answered.

She returned in a few minutes with a piece of notepaper, pointedly monogrammed JFB—there was no P to be found—with a name, address, and phone number on it. I thanked her and headed back to the car.

The piece of paper said "Pat (Johnson) Moody," and gave a Ridgefield address.

I mentally moved Joyce Branscomb down to the bottom of my list, joining Priscilla Hampden. If she'd been singing and dancing in The Fantasticks in 1966, and understudying the lead, she wasn't having a baby. Such a combination might just be conceivable in 1996, but it certainly wasn't in 1966. Of course, there was also the possibility that her story was false, but I could always check it out later if I had to.

RELATIVE TO WHERE I was, Ridgefield was sort of a "you can't get there from here" proposition, but I supposed not being at the crossroads of the world was one of its charms, and I found my way there eventually.

Ridgefield had grown considerably in the twenty-some years since I had last been there, but the house I was seeking was old—a rambling, comfortable-looking shingle with a big, covered porch. The porch held an old-fashioned glider that I knew would squeak unbearably if you sat in it and the kind of wicker chairs that I always associated, because of some faintly remembered scene in a movie, with Sydney Greenstreet.

As I was coming up the walk, a robust and athletic-looking woman came out on the porch, accompanied by a pair of dachshunds who eyed me warily. I regretted that Molly wasn't with me, because dachsies always made her feel so tall.

She spoke first, saying, "Are you the woman Joyce Branscomb just called me about?"

"Yes, I am. Lexy Connor," I said, extending my hand to her.

"I'm Pat Moody," she said, accepting my handshake. "Come on in. I was just having some iced tea. Would you like some?" I said I would, and sat down at the big kitchen table she motioned me to.

Like the outside of the house, everything inside was spacious and comfortable, although not at all luxurious.

"Joyce said you had some story about a lost ring or something. That you were looking for PJs."

I nodded. "That's right—the ring has the initials PJ inscribed inside."

She shook her head. "It's not mine, or at least not that I recall. Why is it so important? Is it valuable?"

"I don't think so. It's important because I think it would have great sentimental significance to the owner."

"Significant enough to go driving all over Connecticut on a Sunday afternoon?"

"It's a lovely day for a drive, and there isn't any place to do it prettier than Connecticut."

She laughed at that.

Pat Moody was a talker, and I'd caught her on an afternoon with no one to talk to. I was it. I privately suspected that she had had a large family largely to forestall having this problem very often. Fortunately, she was a reasonably interesting talker, and I've spent many a worse afternoon. Somewhere in the course of it, I learned that among her seven children, one was a boy born in the fall of 1966. All the talking in the world wasn't going to produce one child in the summer of 1966 and another in the fall. She wasn't the PJ I was looking for.

TWELVE

I STARTED ON the dreaded phone calls that evening. For the most part, when someone did answer, the conversation was short and simple.

"I'm trying to locate the Patricia Jackson who graduated from Kingsbridge High School in Larchmont, New York, in the late 'fifties or early 'sixties."

"Sorry, not me."

I quickly learned to withhold the specific year of graduation as a way of testing those people who thought it would be interesting to claim to be the person I was seeking.

I got more answering machines than answering people, but I didn't leave any messages. How could anyone try to call me back when I had the phone in constant use? Sometimes I would forget what number I was calling and what PJ I was calling about, which led to some befuddlement and did not add to my pleasure in the task.

On Monday, there were more answering machines to deal with, to the point where I determined that normal working hours were not going to be productive hours for me, except that I had nothing else to do but this. In the early afternoon, I called Bruce Morita in hopes he'd solved his murder case and could give me a reason to stop making all these phone calls, but no such luck. They had made no more progress than I had, except to eliminate from consideration the people who hadn't shown up for their reservations at the San Carlos Court. In the late afternoon, I took a break and drove to Tenafly again in pursuit of Pamela Stuart. There was still no one at the house, or at least no one who would answer the door.

By Tuesday afternoon, my weekend success began to look like the end of my luck. Still, I had connected with less than a sixth of the names on my call list, so as much as I wanted to, I didn't let myself quit. I didn't even take another trip to Tenafly, and was munching my deli sandwich dinner when I suddenly actually connected with Patricia Jacobs. I had to swallow quickly and take a swig of my Fresca before I could make my little speech.

"I'm trying to locate the Patricia Jacobs who graduated from Jefferson High School in White Plains in the early 'sixties."

"Yeah."

"Do you mind my asking what year you graduated?"

"In nineteen sixty-two. But this is the last time I'm going to tell you, I'm not interested in that reunion thing. I didn't like all those bitches then and I sure as hell wouldn't like them now."

"Oh, this isn't about any reunion. I'm calling about another matter altogether."

"What?"

"Well, it involves some lost property that might belong to you. Could I come and see you?"

There was a long hesitation.

"What property?"

"I'd really prefer to discuss it in person, if I may."

"Look, if you think you can scam me with one of those deals where I pay you to tell me how to get my money, you've got another think coming."

"No, I promise you I will never ask for a cent. But I would like to talk to you in person."

"Well, not tonight. I can't tonight."

"Tomorrow?"

"In the evening, I guess would be okay. After eight o'clock. Don't come before eight." She gave me an address near Valhalla, a community that consists mostly of cemeteries. It is northwest of White Plains, out past the Kensico Reservoir Dam.

I tried to convince myself that finding Patricia Jacobs meant that I didn't have to make any more phone calls until after I'd eliminated her from consideration, but I didn't do a very good job of it, so I hit the phones some more.

PATRICIA JACOBS lived in a ramshackle, featureless little house, badly in need of some basic maintenance. When she came to the door, I couldn't help but think that the house and its tenant were made for each other, and then silently chastised myself for making judgments on appearances. She stepped out onto the tiny porch and closed the door behind her, meanwhile holding a finger to her lips in a gesture meant to keep me silent.

"My boyfriend," she whispered. "I thought he'd be gone by now, but he's not working tonight after all. I don't want him to know about this." She grabbed my arm and led me away from the house, back to the street, and behind a large bush where we couldn't be seen from the front windows of the house.

"Okay," she said, looking back toward the house over her shoulder, "he can't see us here. What kind of property?"

"A ring," I said.

"A ring? Yeah, yeah, it's mine. I lost it last week. Give it to me now. He'll kill me if he finds out I lost it." She looked back over her shoulder again, as if in fear that he was on his way out to kill her now.

"I can't give it to you unless I'm sure it's yours. Can you describe it?"

"Well, it's a ring. You know, with a jewel and everything." She now looked back at me, frantic for some clue in my face as to what the ring looked like.

"What kind of jewel?"

"Diamonds. A great big one and a bunch of little ones." She took a shot in the dark, but she certainly wasn't thinking small.

"I'm terribly sorry about your loss, Ms. Jacobs, but that's not the ring I have, and I've had it for longer than a week."

"Maybe it was longer ago than a week that I lost it."

"But the ring I have doesn't have any diamonds."

"Well, then it's the other one I lost, the one I lost before. When did you find it?"

I was thoroughly disgusted by now, but I couldn't just walk away without making sure that this monstrosity of a person wasn't Tally's mother. I gagged at the thought.

"In the summer of nineteen sixty-six," I answered, watching closely for any sign that the date had any significance for her.

"Yeah, that's when I lost the other one," she said, nodding vigorously.

"And can you describe that one?" I asked.

"It only had one big jewel," she said.

"What kind of a jewel?"

"A sapphire."

I wondered for a moment if it was remotely possible she'd think any blue stone was a sapphire. My indecision must have shown in my face, because she went on to say, "That's right, a sapphire—my birthstone—way back in 'sixty-six," and she grinned at me, thinking she'd hit paydirt.

"What was the inscription?" I asked. She peered at my face again, looking for another clue.

"You're just trying to trick me. There was no inscrip—what you said. There wasn't anything written on it when I lost it. If there's something written on it, you wrote it there."

"I'm terribly sorry, but the ring I have isn't the one you lost," I said, and I started to turn away.

"Look," she said, "nineteen sixty-six is too long ago. How can you expect me to remember what was written on it after so long?"

"Okay, then, just tell me what else you lost at the same time that you lost the ring and it's yours."

"What do you mean?"

"I mean that whoever it is the ring belongs to also lost something else very valuable at the same time."

"In nineteen sixty-six? What are you trying to do to me? You know where I was in nineteen sixty-six."

I shook my head, "No, I don't have any idea. Suppose you tell me."

She grabbed my arm and said, "It's my ring. Give me the damn ring, or I'll call Billy and he'll take it off you."

"He'd be wasting his time. I don't have it with me. Besides, the ring isn't worth more than a hundred dollars or so. Do you want to go to jail for assault for a hundred dollars?"

She let go of my arm. "Look, I did my time and that's all over. That's where I was in nineteen sixty-six, if you really want to know. Bedford Hills. Hell, all I want is my ring back. You probably stole it while I was in there. I could use a hundred bucks. You don't know that it's not my ring. You could give it to me; you don't need it. I really need that ring.'' There was now a desperation in her voice that I suspected was never far below the surface of her life.

''It's not your ring,'' I repeated. The wind went out of her and she just looked at me, defeated.

''I'm sorry to have bothered you,'' I said. I turned and walked away again, this time unmolested.

On the drive back to the hotel, I had to work on resolving my mixed feelings of disgust and anger and pity. Ultimately, pity prevailed, but it was a struggle. At the core of all this was the niggling little thought that I hadn't actually eliminated her as a candidate. It wasn't out of the question that she could have been in Bedford Hills, a state prison for women—although I think that nowadays they may call it something on the order of a ''correctional facility''—and still have borne a child. On the other hand, I hadn't actually eliminated any of the other PJs, either, except that they had plausible stories that could be checked out if the time came to do that. Still, Patricia Jacobs hadn't seemed to know anything about the real ring. I would take that as conclusive for the time being. And if I had to, I figured there'd be a way to find out if she'd had a child in Bedford Hills.

THE NEXT DAY, I tackled the phone again. I had now made contact with fully a quarter of the names on my call list. It had taken two days to find Patricia Jacobs;

maybe the others were out there to be found if I just kept at it.

Even though it cut into my prime calling time, I decided to visit Tenafly again, this time at a later hour than before. When I pulled up outside the house, I was encouraged to find lamps lit at several front windows.

An elderly woman answered the door, opening it only as wide as the chain allowed. "I'm looking for Pamela Stuart," I said.

"My daughter is still in the hospital," she answered. "I only just got back from there."

"Oh, I'm sorry, I didn't know. Is it serious?"

"They don't know. They really don't know anything about this. And we'd been doing so well for so long, we'd put it all behind us. The years in the iron lung, the braces, the wheelchair, the pain, and now it's all back."

"Post-polio syndrome?" I asked, and she nodded wearily.

The polio epidemics of the 'forties and 'fifties had cast a long shadow over my childhood and that of my contemporaries. We were enthralled and terrified by the horror stories of children being suddenly stricken with paralysis after a day at the neighborhood swimming pool. In the worst years, some swimming pools shut down in the peak season, but staying away from swimming pools wasn't enough to guarantee your safety. Then in the mid-'fifties came the Salk vaccine and, as we lined up to get our treated sugar cubes, we congratulated ourselves that we were now beyond the reach of this scourge. Over the succeeding years, we heard stories of gutsy patients, unlucky enough to have contracted the disease before Salk, gradually overcoming its more debilitating aspects and coming to lead near-normal lives.

Near normal until about ten or fifteen years ago, that is, when post-polio syndrome began to show up in the survivors, delivering chronic pain and fatigue upon its victims once again. I didn't know any more about it than that.

"I'm so sorry," I said. "Look, I really don't want to bother you, but I have to ask just one question. I'm looking for a woman with the initials 'PJ' who had a baby girl in the summer of nineteen sixty-six. Could it possibly be your daughter?"

She shook her head slowly but emphatically. "She was living with me in nineteen sixty-six, and I guarantee you she didn't have any baby. She was practically a baby herself, she needed so much help."

"Thank you. I'm sorry to have troubled you; you certainly have enough to deal with as it is."

"It was no trouble," she said wearily. Then her face brightened and she said, "But there is something you can do for me. I don't drive now and I forgot to get something I needed before the volunteer who drives me dropped me off from the hospital. I didn't want to call her to come back because she lives twenty miles from here, but since you're here, could you take me to the supermarket for my prescription? I really do need it tonight and it's only a few miles."

"I'd be more than delighted to," I answered.

On our little junket, I told her a little about my quest, leaving out all the scary parts, and she told me about Pamela and kept repeating to me what a nice girl I was to take her to the market. I bought some flowers for her to take to Pamela the next day, and was told again what a nice girl I was. After I helped her get her purchases into the house and expressed the hope that Pamela's condition would improve, I went off with her thanks ringing in my ears. As I headed back toward Westchester, I speculated, not for the first time, on how I would deal with it when it came time—if I lasted that long—to surrender my car keys and my automobility. I didn't think I would handle it well and wondered if I shouldn't start thinking seriously of becoming a city dweller once more.

WHEN I FINALLY got back from Tenafly, I had to stop and consider what I was doing. In a week, I had located and, for all practical purposes, eliminated five of my fifteen, but I also knew that I had already plucked the low-hanging fruit. From now on, each successive name would take a much greater effort to track down than the preceding one. More important, the process I was following, if it could even be called that, was only going to lead me to people who were among the living. There was no reason to believe that Tally's mother was alive. In fact, if I were to bet, I would have bet she wasn't. I felt certain that she would have surfaced long since if she were alive. Not only that, I couldn't imagine Susan and Peter conspiring to keep a child hidden away from its natural mother, and they had almost certainly conspired to keep her hidden away from someone.

THIRTEEN

"I'M GOING TO HIRE a private eye. I need a professional," I had said to Tally on the phone the night before.

"That's what expense accounts are for," she had answered, laughing.

I needed a professional, but I had no more idea than the man in the moon how one went about selecting a private investigator. As nearly as I could tell from half a century of reading crime fiction, every private eye who wasn't the hero of the book was a sleaze-bag. Then I remembered the retired judge Hunter had told me to call if I needed help; this ought to be right up his alley. I dug around in my haphazard notes until I found his name and number.

A woman answered the phone, "Seabrook residence."

"This is Lexy Connor calling. May I speak to Judge Seabrook please?"

"Oh, yes, Ms. Connor. The judge has been expecting your call. Please hold on while I get him."

After a brief wait, the judge picked up the phone.

"Charlie Seabrook here. Hunter told me to expect your call. What can I do for you?"

"I need a referral for a private detective," I answered.

"That's easy enough. Call Pratt & Hirsch in White Plains and ask for Sophie Hirsch. She's honest, efficient, and discreet. Use my name as a reference and you'll get her personal attention."

"I can't do better than that."

"But Hunter said you could fill me in on a fascinating story and I'm very bored today and in need of some fascination. Can I take you to dinner?"

After the week I'd just had, an evening of congenial conversation and good food was an offer I couldn't refuse.

"I'd be delighted," I said.

After I'd finished with the judge, I called Sophie Hirsch and luckily caught her at her desk and was able to make an appointment for as fast as I could get there. I didn't doubt for a moment that dropping Judge Seabrook's name was the reason behind my swift entree.

PRATT & HIRSCH WAS located on the top floor of one of the older three-story buildings near the county courthouse in White Plains, the county seat. There was a bail bondsman's office and an attorney's office on the first floor and an insurance claims office on the second floor, so I felt like I was in private eye territory.

I don't know if I was expecting a Kinsey Millhone or a Sharon McCone or a V. I. Warshawski, but Sophie Hirsch was none of these. She was middle-aged, redheaded, well-upholstered, and gave off an air of brusque but not unfriendly self-confidence. She was dressed in a no-nonsense navy blue suit that was of excellent quality but had seen some hard wear. I was to discover that she also had an easy and earthy sense of humor, but at this first meeting it was all business.

"What can we do for you?" she asked after I had been settled in a chair with a cup of coffee.

"I'm trying to locate someone. A woman. That's not quite right. I'm really trying to identify a woman. I have a handful of names here, with everything I know about these names, which isn't much, and the person I'm trying to identify may be one of these names, but I don't even know that for sure. Was that terribly confusing?''

Sophie nodded.

"Let me try again. I am looking for a woman who probably went to high school in Westchester County, graduating somewhere between nineteen fifty-eight and nineteen sixty-two, who had a baby girl in the summer of nineteen sixty-six, possibly out of wedlock, and whose initials are probably 'PJ,' but I don't know if the 'J' is a last name or a middle name." I handed her the list of names, saying, "These names are ranked roughly by probability, with the ten on top being the likeliest candidates and the last five I've pretty much eliminated.''

She looked at the list and then asked, "What is the basis of that probability for the top ten?''

"I think it's likely that the person I'm looking for is dead, and the last five are certainly alive and kicking. I don't know if the first ten are dead or alive.''

"And if the person isn't dead?" she said.

"Then I would like to locate her, but since I think it's likely she's dead, that's where the investigation ought to start.''

"How and when do you think she died?''

"I don't have any idea how, but I think it was probably in nineteen sixty-six.''

"Nineteen sixty-six?" she said, and did a comic double-take. "This is an adoption thing, isn't it?''

"Sort of, but that's confidential.''

"Ms. Connor, everything you tell me is confidential unless it becomes a matter of court order. Our communications are not privileged unless you go through a lawyer.''

"Oh, we don't need to worry about that. In some ways it is a police matter in Los Angeles, but the police there are focusing on something else—a crime that happened there a few weeks ago,'' I responded.

"Should I be concerned about that aspect of it?'' she asked.

"Not at the moment. In fact, LAPD has made a decision not to notify any police agency in Westchester County about this inquiry.'' I decided that it probably wouldn't be wise to point out that there'd been some arm-twisting involved, and hoped she wouldn't push it. I didn't mind lying to real estate agents, but your own private eye was another matter altogether, and at the moment I still didn't care to show my entire hand.

She shrugged acceptance. "If any of them are dead and they died in this area, this will be fairly easy and I'll have an answer soon. Those county records are all computerized and go back further than we need them to. How urgent is this?''

"It's fairly urgent. It may even be a matter of life and death—but I hardly like to admit that even to myself.'' I couldn't believe I was hearing myself say that, but then I thought about Dolly Miller again and I knew it was, in a way at least, true.

"Okay, I'll get right on it. Fortunately, I'm free myself this afternoon and any friend of the judge's gets all our attention. I have a great deal of respect for Judge Seabrook. We're strictly time and expenses here, and I can have a standard contract drawn up for you in just a few minutes.''

I thought it was probably not a good time to tell her that I hadn't even met the judge yet. I was certainly milking my scant acquaintanceship among judges for all it was worth.

With the contract signed and a retainer deposited, I was done at Pratt & Hirsch and walked out into a beautiful September afternoon. But it was wasted on me—I was too preoccupied with thoughts of Tally, Susan, and Dolly. And I couldn't help but think that Susan would be laughing at me if she knew just what a stew she'd landed me in.

I picked up Molly to take her for a walk. Now that she had strolled through Beverly Hills, it seemed appropriate to take a stroll through the residential areas of the Westchester Country Club, little changed in the forty-some years since I'd first seen it.

When we got back to the hotel, there was a message from Sophie Hirsch with a number and a note to call at any time.

When I reached her, she said, "I've found death certificates for two of your first ten."

"Which ones are they?"

"The first one is Patricia Jackson, Larchmont. She died of breast cancer in nineteen sixty-three."

"'Sixty-three is too early; she can't be the one. But breast cancer? She could only have been in her early twenties."

"It happens. I lost a cousin to it who was only nineteen. I have a more promising one, though—she died in the summer of nineteen sixty-six."

"Summer of 'sixty-six? That fits. Which one is it?"

"Paula Jordan Chandler, White Plains. She died on June fifth, nineteen sixty-six."

"June of 'sixty-six?"

"Yes, June fifth."

I gasped a little at that. Tally couldn't have been more than a few weeks old.

"She could be the one I'm looking for. How did she die?" I asked.

"Massive injuries in an automobile accident."

"Automobile accident?" Somehow that was not what I had imagined, although I wasn't certain what I *had* imagined.

"You're surprised that it was an automobile accident?" she asked.

"Well, yes. I'm not sure what I was expecting to hear, but it wasn't a traffic accident," I answered. "If she's the one, maybe even murder," I added.

If this answer surprised Sophie, her voice didn't show it. "Evidently not, or at least the county coroner didn't think so. Do you want me to get a copy of the accident report?" she asked.

"Yes, I suppose we ought to have all the details we can get," I said.

"Good. Finding the record of her death was too easy and I was going to be embarrassed at taking your money. Getting the accident record will take more effort and a little longer, because those records are still paper files and I won't be able to get to that office until they open again on Monday."

"All right. Do it."

"Do you want me to continue to look for the other ones?" she asked.

"No," I said, "let's concentrate on Chandler for the time being. If we eliminate her, then we can go back and look at the others some more."

"I had copies of the death certificates faxed to the hotel for you, but I instructed them not to give them to you until you asked because I wanted to be sure I talked to you first.''

''That was very thoughtful of you,'' I said.

I retrieved the faxed death certificates from the hotel desk, but they added no information to what I'd already learned from Sophie. I studied the yearbook picture of Paula Jordan Chandler, but the quality was so poor that I couldn't judge anything from it except that there was a faint resemblance.

I WAS SO WORN DOWN from all of the week's happenings that I nearly called the judge to cancel our dinner engagement—I didn't think I'd be very good company. I was glad later that I hadn't.

When he arrived to pick me up, I was dressed in my mainstay navy silk blazer, cream silk blouse, and camel slacks. I figured if it didn't get me thrown out of the Beverly Wilshire, I could get away with it country dining in Westchester.

Judge Charles Seabrook had a rosy complexion and silvery white hair and, when he smiled, which seemed to be often, his eyes closed to little slits. With the addition of a beard and mustache, he could have been everyone's favorite Santa. He had an easy laugh that rounded out the picture.

He picked me up in a chauffeured car but was quick to point out that this was not normal. ''Mike,'' he said, pointing to the chauffeur, ''is our designated driver. I'm in the mood for some good wine, and I'll bet you are, too.''

I was later to learn that Mike was half of ''Mike and Martha,'' the live-in couple who'd been taking care of the judge for some twenty years.

He took me to a country inn not far from where

Hawthorne Circle used to be. The restaurant was lovely—a big old frame house with subdued lighting and a hostess who fawned over the judge. The tables were laden with fresh flowers and crystal that shimmered in the candlelight. Classical music played softly in the background, and the menu was as big as a highway atlas.

Of course, I had to tell him the whole story, right up to the telephone call to Tally just a few hours earlier. He was attentive, sympathetic, charming, and funny. I fell in love.

When I told him of my plan to search for newspaper accounts of Paula Chandler's accident while waiting for Sophie to turn up the police report, he said, "Let me make it easier for you," and pulled a cell phone out of his pocket.

I must have made a face, because he said, "It wasn't turned on. I carry it for *my* convenience, no one else's." I laughed at that because he'd read my mind.

He dialed a number from the phone memory, and, after some friendly exchanges having to do with golf games and sailing, said, "Hank, I need a favor. I have a friend who needs access to the morgue in White Plains tomorrow to do some research. Can you arrange that?"

He paused for a moment and then looked at me and said, "Is ten o'clock all right?"

I nodded, still not quite sure what I was supposed to be doing at ten o'clock.

He went on with his conversation, saying, "Lexy Connor. She's staying at the Hutch Heights; you can leave word there."

After a few more civilities, the conversation ended and I was able to ask, "What morgue?"

"Sterling's," he answered, and it all became clear. Sterling had started with one local paper in Westchester County many years before, and while it was now a major media force throughout the country, it still held firm to its Westchester roots.

Once more, I was to experience the privileges of being well-connected. From the bottom of my plebeian soul, I didn't mind at all.

Back at the hotel, I found a faxed note telling me to meet with Celie Johnson at the Sterling Westchester office any time after ten o'clock the next day.

FOURTEEN

I WAS AWAKENED the next morning by room service bringing my breakfast and two dozen Tropicana roses with a card that said, "I cannot wait until a decent hour to learn if you'll have dinner with me tonight; please call earliest. Charlie."

I looked at Molly and said, "Good grief, we're being courted."

Since I have no objections whatsoever to being courted, I called and accepted the invitation. I also decided that I needed something new to wear and that this was as good an excuse as I was going to get to visit Saks Fifth Avenue in Westchester. Saks had discovered a few years earlier that fat women have money to spend on clothes, too, so it was now possible for me to find something to wear there.

But first things first. At ten o'clock I presented myself at Sterling Media National Headquarters on Westchester Avenue and was met in the lobby by a stunning young woman who introduced herself as Celie Johnson, head research librarian. Sleekly groomed and dressed in haute career couture, she was a startling change from the librarians I'd dealt with the week before last.

"I'm sorry to bring you in on a weekend," I began, thinking to protest my innocence.

"Don't be concerned about that," she answered. "Newspapers are a seven-day-a-week business and I was going to be here anyway. And I love the opportunity to do a personal favor for Mr. Sterling—he always remembers when you do.''

So Judge Seabrook's "Hank" was "Mr. Sterling." (Despite the two dozen roses and instructions to call him "Charlie," I still thought of him as "Judge Seabrook," although at the present rate, I didn't think I would much longer.)

She led me back through several corridors and into a library and then into an office inside the library and flipped on a muscular-looking workstation.

"Okay," she said, "what are we after?"

"We're after everything we can find out about a fatal traffic accident thirty years ago."

"Wonderful!" she exclaimed. "The old ones are such a challenge because the data collection was so iffy back then. Even the *New York Times* didn't get its morgue on-line until the late 'sixties, and it was the very first. The legacy data is pretty much of a hodge-podge." I decided not to indulge myself by telling any of the war stories associated with the *New York Times* and its automation of its morgue, especially as it had happened before she was born and she clearly thought of it as ancient history.

"What are the particulars?" she asked.

"The date of the accident was five June 'sixty-six, probably somewhere in Westchester County, and the name of the person killed was Paula Chandler."

She jotted these down on a notepad, and then began her search. In a matter of seconds she had a hit. "Scanned," she muttered as the display started to paint a smudgy, broken image of the article. "The quality won't be too good because the scanners used to scan legacy data in the 'eighties just weren't that good," she said to me. "Let me see if my optical reader software can convert it to something more legible."

She poked and prodded at a few more things and a new version of the article, now highly readable, began to paint on the screen.

"Now there's a technology that's come a long way," I said as I watched.

"It's pretty amazing if you know what's involved. People who don't know how difficult it is aren't impressed, I'm afraid. The software doesn't do as well on random materials, but it is highly tuned for the fonts that were actually used in the papers, and what it can't read it makes educated guesses about. When we find something that it hasn't handled right, we can 'teach' it to handle it right the next time, so over the years it's become pretty refined. It hardly ever fails on straight news stories now except where the original was really bad or the scan really skewed."

I read the story over her shoulder.

Traffic Accident Claims Two Area Residents

June 5, 1966, White Plains—A late night collision on the Taconic Parkway claimed two area residents early this morning. Dead at the scene were Paula Jordan Chandler, 23, recently of White Plains, and Lawrence Foster Prescott III, 30, of Larchmont.

The accident occurred just south of the Putnam-Westchester border at approximately 3AM. The State Highway Patrol is asking that any witnesses come forward.

The investigating officers believe that Prescott, driving a Mercedes-Benz sedan, fell asleep at the

wheel and struck the Alfa Romeo driven by Miss
Chandler from behind. Both cars left the road and
were destroyed at the scene. The drivers were
thrown from their cars and killed instantly. There
were no other passengers in either car.

Miss Chandler graduated from Jefferson High
School in White Plains and Katherine Gibbs in
New York City and, until recently, had lived in
White Plains all her life. She had been employed
as a secretary in White Plains by the public relations firm Bartlett & Ruskie, but left there several
months ago for opportunities in the Albany area.

Mr. Prescott was a partner in the well-known
Wall Street law firm, Burns, Prescott & Prescott.
He was a graduate of Larchmont Country Day
School and Princeton University and received his
law degree from Yale University. He resided with
his wife, Clarissa Fillmore Prescott, and father,
Lawrence Foster Prescott II, in Larchmont.

She looked up at me and said, "Is that the one?"

"That's the one," I said. Just a stupid traffic accident. So tragic and so banal.

"That icon there means there are pictures, too. Want
to see them?"

I nodded that I did.

A venetian-blind image began to paint and repaint
on the screen. "We display them in interlaced form for
use on the web," Celie said as the image was repainted
with greater detail each time. "Someone calling in
from a remote location can tell pretty quickly if the
picture is the one they want with this technique, without having to wait until the whole thing is down-
loaded."

The first picture was a studio portrait of him, but that was quickly followed by a studio portrait of her and, in spite of the poor quality of the reproduction, I knew instantly who I was looking at. I must have gasped because Celie looked at me sharply.

"That's her, that's got to be her," I said. I was looking at Tally's face in a portrait taken before she was born. The Paula Chandler high school yearbook photo, taken some years earlier and possibly some thirty pounds heavier, had not shown me this.

"Let's look for follow-ups," she said. "There were probably obits, and if he was a high muckety-muck Wall Street lawyer, the *New York Times* and the *Wall Street Journal* will probably have some stuff on him, too."

"I'm not much interested in him, but let's see what else you have on her."

"I'm going to pull everything on both of them," she responded. "The cross-indexing done on the legacy documents was such that if the story mentioned both of them and only he was prominent, she might not get indexed, so I make it a habit to pull everything that might be remotely related. We do much better with the newer material because we have full text search, but for those days we have to rely on what entry clerks thought was important."

The next hit on the list was a major story about his funeral, in which the accident and the involvement of Paula Chandler were mentioned in passing.

The printer started a steady whirring and clicking as Celie ordered prints of each story in turn.

Next came Paula's obit.

PAULA JORDAN CHANDLER, 23

Beloved daughter of Lucille Jordan Chandler and the late Paul F. Chandler of White Plains, killed in a traffic accident on June 5, 1966. A life-long resident of White Plains until recently, Miss Chandler graduated from White Plains' Jefferson High School in 1961 and from Katherine Gibbs in New York City in 1963.

    She is survived by her mother, Lucille, of White Plains, and a sister, Lucille Chandler (Mrs. Randolph) Baker, of Portchester, New York.

No mention of a child, which was no surprise. Her departure for "other opportunities" in Albany didn't fool me. In 1966, the Pill was available but its use was considered proof of scandalous intent, the landmark Supreme Court decision on abortion was still seven years in the future, and middle class unwed mothers bore their children away from the prying eyes of friends and neighbors.

Celie was reading the obit along with me, and barely suppressed a giggle.

"What's making you laugh?" I asked.

"Lucille Chandler Baker," she answered. "All she needs now is a butcher."

As she had predicted, there were *New York Times* and *Wall Street Journal* obits on Prescott, but nothing more about Paula.

"Evidently there weren't any lawsuits," Celie said as she scanned the hits for Prescott.

"Lawsuits?" I said.

"Yes, wrongful death. It looks to me as if they had a pretty good case against Prescott."

"It was a little different thirty years ago. People still thought tragic accidents were acts of God and not opportunities for the enrichment of the survivors. A minor gesture like paying for the funeral was considered generous."

"There is something to be said for that," she said.

"There is a great deal to be said for that," I answered.

"What else?" she asked after she had pulled the Prescott articles down and printed them.

"A shot in the dark. Do you have anything on a Dolores or Dolly Morgan?"

"Old or new?"

"Old."

There were zero hits for that one, so I tried another.

"How about Bartlett and Ruskie, the company Paula worked for? This time search back from today rather than forward from 'sixty-six. I'd like to know if they're still around."

She keyed a few more search arguments.

"Nope. Sold by the widow of the founding partner in nineteen eighty-five, it says here."

Without being asked, she went ahead and searched on Burns, Prescott & Prescott; they had been merged out of existence in the early 'eighties, upon the retirement of the senior Prescott.

"Apparently he's still around; there's no obit on him," Celie reported as she read through the hit list one more time.

"Here's an obit on Paula's mother, though," she said as she completed another search. "Died last year. And the sister was still alive then, but it shows her in New Rochelle instead of Portchester. Let's see if she's listed," she said as she pulled up a national phone directory in another window.

"Bingo. Forty Calton Street. Want a map?"

"Sure. Why not?" I answered and she hit a few more buttons to bring up a street map of the area in New Rochelle that held 40 Calton Street.

As she routed the map to the printer, she turned around to me with a big grin and said, "God, I love this. I don't usually get that much chance to play with the toys any more. This has been fun."

"Well, it certainly beats sitting at a microfiche machine scrolling through ancient microfilm, let alone plowing through paper files."

"I should hope to think so. And there was so much human effort wasted that way for so many years. When the morgue here was still in paper, the guess was that about fifty percent of the material was misfiled or otherwise unlocatable. And then for a long time the price of storage was so high no one but the *New York Times* could afford to put full text of current material on-line, let alone legacy data."

"The *Times* always thought it had the only morgue worth putting on-line," I said.

"There's probably a lot of truth in that. Still, even here people come looking for the strangest things after thirty years." She looked up at me archly.

"And there's a lot of truth in that, too," I acknowledged in return.

"Is there anything else we can do today?"

"Is it possible to get print files for those articles? I'd like to upload them so I can transmit them to the west coast."

"Of course. Is PostScript okay?"

"PostScript is perfect."

"I can give them to you on a diskette," she said, "but if you're just going to ship them anyway, why don't I just put them in your own directory on an FTP site for you and your people on the west coast can download them from there."

"That would be perfect," I said. In a few moments, she had accomplished that task.

"Anything else?" she asked.

"I can't think of anything. You've been a tremendous help."

"Well, if you think of anything else, our services are at your disposal. If you're on the Net, I can ship you anything you need, but I'll also authorize you to do your own searches. Please feel free to call me at any time; this number will always reach me and I always have a workstation with me," she said as she gave me her card.

"Always?" I said.

"Almost always, although they still haven't made a waterproof one I can take in the shower."

"You're the second nerd I've met recently who doesn't look like a nerd. What's going on with the nerds of the world?"

"It's our secret takeover conspiracy," she answered with a laugh. "Now please let me take you to lunch in our executive dining room as Mr. Sterling's guest."

That seemed like a good idea to me and so I did. I had to admire Celie's professional cool; if she had any curiosity at all about my quest, she didn't show it.

An hour and an excellent lobster salad (real Maine lobster in recognizable chunks) later, I was headed the short distance to Saks Fifth Avenue. I'd tried the Randolph Baker number in New Rochelle while still in Celie's office, but got an answering machine and since

I had no idea how to present myself in such a way as to get a call back, I didn't leave a message.

Staying out of Saks—or any place like it—had been one of the necessary economies of my not-terribly-successful self-employment, but a few weeks on Tally's payroll made it possible to consider a visit, if not a resumption of the habit. I've always loved shopping at Saks. While some of their designer-label merchandise gets into the stratospheric ranges, the fact is you don't pay any more at Saks for merchandise comparable to what you can find in another store, the merchandise is always excellent quality for its price, and the service is always superb. And they have sales just like everybody else.

The Westchester Saks store isn't very large, so the fat lady department, known for some mysterious reason as "Salon Z," is tiny, but it must have had a simpatico buyer, because I saw several things I lusted after. I finally settled on a pair of dark navy douppioni silk wide-leg pants with a matching jacket, coordinated with a silk jacquard tee in bright yellow. I felt a twinge of guilt at the yards of douppioni gathering dust in my fabric stash in Colorado, but they were there and I was here and the need was immediate. On impulse, I grabbed a black silk shantung outfit that was on sale and added it to my pile at the last minute. You can never have too many black silk shantung outfits.

The success of my shopping venture put me in a positive frame of mind as I headed back to the Hutch Heights, as Charlie had called it, to take Molly for her walk and touch base with California, read my e-mail, and try again to reach Lucille Baker in New Rochelle.

FIFTEEN

AFTER THE INITIAL elation of finding Tally's mother—at a point when I was about to give up the idea that I actually would—I felt a sharp letdown. I still didn't know what I needed to know to protect Tally. Finding a name to put to the PJ in Dolly's note and in the ring had become an objective all its own, but it didn't make Tally any safer. Indeed, having made a connection, however tenuous, between Tally and Paula Chandler, I may have increased the risk, although I wasn't sure how.

WHEN I GOT TO the hotel, I sucked up my courage and called Tally.

"I've identified her, without any doubt. You are her spitting image." I said.

"Who is it?"

"Paula Jordan Chandler, class of 'sixty-one, Jefferson High in White Plains. She was killed in a car accident in June of 'sixty-six."

"Anything else?" she said after a long pause.

"Her yearbook entry says French club, drama club, dean's list, National Honor Society, and her obit says Katie Gibbs and then she worked for a public relations firm in White Plains."

"Who's Katie Gibbs?"

"Katie Gibbs, or, more properly, Katherine Gibbs, was and probably still is a high-class secretarial school, the Harvard of secretarial schools. It was a very select and respectable place to be in the 'sixties."

"My mother was a secretary?" she said.

"Hey, that was the entry point for a business career for women in those days. You didn't go to B school and get your MBA first; you went to work and hoped you'd make a good enough impression to be plucked out of the typing pool for something better. Offices were full of secretaries who were ten times smarter and more qualified than the people they made coffee for. I only escaped it myself because I couldn't take shorthand."

"Okay, okay—my snobbery was showing."

"Not your snobbery, dear—your failure to appreciate what life was like for the generations before the feminist revolution. For instance, if your real goal was to be an editor in a publishing house, you went to an Ivy League Sister School, got a bachelor's degree in English, and then went to secretarial school to learn typing and shorthand so you could get an entry-level job in the typing pool in a publishing house. Publishing was a glamour industry and an employer's market, so they paid dirt. If you were interested in economics and finance, you became a bank teller. It wasn't a glamour industry and they paid dirt, too."

Tally sighed. She'd heard this lecture before; unlike others of her generation, she'd never been allowed to take for granted what her mother's generation had gained for women who wanted choices in their lives.

"I think you have an aunt in New Rochelle," I said. "I've been trying to get in touch with her, but so far I haven't been successful."

"What are you going to tell her?"

"I'm going to use a variation on the *New Yorker* profile story—it's worked so far."

"You're not going to tell her about me?"

"There'll be time enough for that when we know everything we need to know to remove the threat to you."

"I suppose that's true. Let's just hope she doesn't have any traffic accidents in the meantime." I could hear bitterness in her voice, so I knew that the day's news was taking its toll.

"We'll figure it out. I promise," I said, wondering where I got the gall to make promises I had no way of knowing whether I could keep or not.

We talked for a long time. The conversation was more difficult than either of us had anticipated it would be. We both mourned this woman we had never known and who had been dead for more than thirty years. But at least Tally knew now, for whatever comfort that might be worth, that her mother hadn't abandoned her.

WHEN I CALLED Santa Barbara, Hunter answered the phone. I told him that I had just had to inform Tally that her birth mother was dead and gave him a quick rundown on what I'd found out.

"She needs family at a time like this," Hunter answered. "We'll go up to Palo Alto tonight."

"I'd certainly appreciate that. I'd fly back, but there's still work to be done here. Knowing who her mother is, or rather was, doesn't solve the problem of where the danger to Tally lies."

Hunter replied "Don't worry, we'll take care of things at this end. Under the circumstances, you and Florrie and I are the only ones she can talk to about this until you get it solved."

I liked his confidence that I would get it solved, but I wasn't sure I shared it.

"Thank you for the referral to Judge Seabrook," I said. "He's been invaluable."

"Well, you better watch out for him. He called me up today and said he was sending me a case of Dom Perignon in gratitude for sending you his way. He said he hasn't enjoyed himself so much in years."

"Wow. Is he dangerous?"

"I told him if he wasn't a perfect gentleman I would personally beat him black and blue."

"But I'm not sure I want him to be a perfect gentleman."

"I'll leave that for the two of you to work out. What else do you have?"

"I have a newspaper account of the accident and her obit, with a picture. She looks just like Tally. That's why I'm so sure she's the right one. There appears to be a sister living in New Rochelle. I've been trying to reach her, but so far I haven't been successful. And I need to use a cover story, too. She may be the enemy." I gulped at that; I had just put into words a thought I hadn't allowed myself to think before.

"Not another *New Yorker* profile?" Hunter said, at which point Florrie broke in to say that she had just joined our conversation on an extension and was hoping this meant she could resume her career with the *New Yorker*.

"No, not another *New Yorker* profile; probably the same *New Yorker* profile. It's worked so far—people around here pay attention when you say 'the *New Yorker*.' In Boulder, you'd have to use *Sports Illustrated* to get the same level of attention. Anyway, I may be about to stick my head above the foxhole, and

I thought someone ought to know what's going on just in case I have a sudden heart attack in my hotel room.''

"I don't like the sound of that," Florrie said. "Maybe it's time to bring the police in."

"Bring them in to do what? The only crime that's been committed was in LA, and the police already have that. Besides, we still haven't eliminated the possibility that the man who was with Dolly Miller when she died was a cop and probably a Westchester cop."

"Why not put your private investigator on it?" Hunter asked.

"I can't do that without telling the private investigator what I'm looking for, and I'm not sure I can answer that question myself. Not only that, the only person here who knows why I'm here is Charlie Seabrook, and I'd like to keep it that way as long as I can. If I have to be careful of anything, it's of letting people know why I'm here."

SEVERAL MORE TRIES at calling Lucille Baker got the answering machine each time, and it occurred to me that perhaps she screened her calls this way, as I often did myself, figuring that anyone I actually wanted to talk to would be someone who'd leave a message.

In between calls, I penned a note to Hank Sterling thanking him for allowing me the use of Celie Johnson and her miracle machine. After all, I might want to use that connection again and I had long since learned that thank-you notes sent in the right direction could do wonders for a person's career as well as earning points for the sender. I imagined Celie's career was going to be quite all right without any help from me, but it couldn't hurt.

Finally I gave up on Lucille and pushed her to the back of my mind, showered, and put on the navy silk.

I loved the way its dull sheen caught and played back the light as only silk does. This called for the Ferragamos, I feared. Fortunately, they were black patent and went with everything. I cheered the day black patent leather was liberated from its never-after-Labor-Day status and was allowed to accompany us year 'round. There was hardly anything it didn't work well with and in a pinch it could be cleaned up with spit on a tissue.

Charlie arrived on the dot of seven and spent several minutes lavishing attention on Molly, playing her own particular version of fetch with a tennis ball. On any number of occasions, I have asked her to pay attention when other dogs play fetch because they have this charming habit of actually dropping the ball, if not in your hand, at least where you can reach it so you can throw it again. Molly thinks this is for wimps and prefers her own technique of returning the ball but then keeping it tantalizingly out of reach when you try to take it to throw again. (It's a terrier thing.) To get her to drop the ball and then push it toward you, you have to pretend a total lack of interest in the game, indicated by exaggeratedly turning your head to the side. This is the same gesture a dog uses to indicate that they don't want any part of something, so it is a language they understand.

Having achieved the approval of my immediate family, Charlie took me out, this time to one of those immense old lobster houses on the Connecticut shore. Lobster twice in one day! I was fairly certain I had died and gone to heaven.

Once the waiter brought our cocktails and left us alone, I said, "I talked to Hunter today and I feel like I'm back in grammar school, when your best friend comes to tell you that a boy in your class says he really likes you."

He laughed and said, "You probably ought to feel that way because that's pretty much the way it is."

"Well, I told my friend to tell the boy that I liked him, too."

"What a relief that is."

"You're sure you're not just a weird guy who digs fat chicks."

"Not to my knowledge."

"Well, if I catch you ogling other fat chicks, you're dog meat," I said.

"Fair enough," he replied, and we both applied ourselves to the menu.

Over the Caesar salad—a real one, not one with bottled "Caesar" dressing—I told him about my day and Celie Johnson, trying to explain why I found the state of the technology so awesome. I think I failed, because to appreciate what is being done today, you have to realize what couldn't be done as recently as ten or even five years ago.

"I wish someone would teach me how to use my computer," Charlie said.

"You don't know how to use it?" I asked.

"I sort of know how to use my word processor and read and write e-mail, but that's it."

"I must know several dozen retired techies within thirty miles of here; I'll find you a tutor," I said. While everyone knows there are techies in Silicon Valley and around Route 128 outside of Boston, few realize just how many of them inhabit Westchester County, despite IBM's having, for decades, been the county's largest private employer.

"How long have you had your system?"

"About five years."

"Well, the first thing they're going to want to do is upgrade you, and you might as well let them, because the software you should be running won't run fast enough to suit you on the machine you have."

"Built-in obsolescence?"

"You could say 'built-in obsolete.' It happens too fast to be mere 'obsolescence.' The day you walk out of the computer store with it, it's over the hill. It's worse than driving a new car off the showroom floor. At least the car still has a dozen years or so of life in it."

"But the computer still works, too," he protested.

"Yes, it still works, but the important thing is what software you can run, and each new version of software requires that much more muscle in the machine you run it on. The software keeps getting sexier all the time, and you wind up having to have all that stuff. You'd be amazed at how much your word processor has improved in those five years. Plus there are a whole bunch of other things besides word processing you'll want to do once you know how. It can balance your checkbook, pay your bills, and check the value of your stock portfolio and tell you your net worth while it's at it."

"Oh, I like that," he said.

"Like today," I said, "Celie, the research librarian, said to the machine 'make this more readable' and it did—bad copies of thirty-year-old newspaper articles, and it made them look like they'd just come out today."

Thinking back to the morning's output from Celie's

system, I asked him, "Did you by any chance know Lawrence Foster Prescott the third?"

"Is that the accident we've been talking about?" he answered.

"I take that to mean you did know him."

"Yes, I did, although not terribly well. His practice was in Manhattan—Wall Street, actually—and mine was in Westchester, so we didn't have much occasion to deal with each other professionally, but I did have contact with him and his wife socially. In fact, I still see her from time to time at charitable functions. I remember going to his funeral; there was an enormous turnout, because of his father as much as anything. I remember his father seemed to be in shock and his widow was completely distraught. A very sad day."

"So his father was a big deal?"

"Oh, yes. There must have been several robber barons in the earlier generations, because there was a great deal of inherited wealth, plus Foster was extremely successful in his own right. Pres was doing well, too, but, being a second-generation partner in a family firm, he hadn't yet proven himself. He can't have been more than in his early thirties when he died."

"Just thirty," I said.

"Yes, I guess that would be about right. It was a long time ago."

"No children, I take it."

"No, no children."

After that, the judge told me about his own children and grandchildren. His daughter was married to a diplomat and lived in one of the marginally safer places in the Middle East. His son was doing bio-chemical research at a major university on the west coast. Charlie had been widowed ten years earlier, when his wife, weakened from a long struggle with multiple sclerosis, succumbed to pneumonia.

Happily, he spared me the indignity of wondering aloud why I had never married; it always amazes me that people think that a reasonable question to ask a woman, as if they had a right to know (and as if the answer were something simple). If a woman has been divorced three times, it's considered rude to ask her why she's such a loser at marriage, but there's no rudeness in asking a woman why she failed utterly in the marriage market in the first place. It is especially obnoxious when it is asked by someone who you know is thinking, "Why didn't anybody ever ask you?" as if asking was getting.

We went on from there to explore our mutual interests, and I couldn't help but notice a tendency to plan our future together, although I wasn't going to take it very seriously. When we concluded that my love for the ballet was equal to or greater than his for the opera, he announced that he would happily go to the ballet often if I would go to the opera occasionally. He was dismayed when I drew the line at having to sit through anything Mozart except for "Eine Kleine Nachtmusik" or the theme from "Elvira Madigan." When I explained that Mozart sets my teeth on edge, he was sympathetic but I think he secretly believed, as most Mozart lovers do, that I simply hadn't had sufficient exposure. There would be time to deal with that if the need ever arose, so I didn't press it.

For several hours that evening I was able to forget about Paula Chandler, Dolly Miller, and the threat to Tally that I still hadn't removed.

We parted with his expressing regret that a previous engagement kept him from spending the next day with me, to which I responded that I was supposed to be doing a job and maybe it would be a good idea if I spent some time on it. When he asked about Monday, I asked if I could let him know on Monday, because my highest priority had to be seeing Lucille Baker, and that was how we left things.

SIXTEEN

THE FLOWERS that arrived with breakfast on Sunday—
an autumnal bouquet in a basket—were accompanied
by a card that read, *These will be the longest two days
of my life.*

"He's getting ridiculous," I said to Molly, but privately I was much flattered by it.

I tried Lucille Baker's phone number again, and
again got the answering machine. I still didn't care to
just leave a message, because I had no way of guar-
anteeing that a message would get me a call back. Having nothing better to do, I decided to go to New Rochelle.

After contemplating the closet for a few minutes, I
decided it was time for one of the power suits, a black
wool number that had carried me in style through many
a client presentation. I carried the Ferragamos, figuring
I could slip them on just before the critical first impression and wouldn't have to totter very far. My usual
footwear is a pair of L.L. Bean's felted wool clogs,
which are more comfortable than wearing nothing at
all, but they don't contribute much to the power image.

It promised to be a cool day, so I took Molly with
me for the fifteen-minute ride down the Hutch.

New Rochelle had somehow managed to miss out
when Westchester County became "hot" for corporate
headquarters relocation in the 'seventies, and its downtown is full of boarded-up storefronts and unsavory-
looking loiterers. To the north and west it was still
comfortably middle-class and prosperous, although not

in the same class with neighboring Scarsdale, Pelham, and Larchmont.

If Tally was right that there was an inheritance somewhere in her background that was worth killing for, it didn't seem likely that this was where it was going to be found.

The address I was seeking was in an older neighborhood. After many years of living in neighborhoods where all the houses had been built within months of one another and to the same six sets of individual floorplans with six variations in the front exterior elevation, it was a pleasure to see the eclectic mix that results from building up a neighborhood over many decades. Some of the houses here were seventy-five or eighty years old, while some others were only ten or twenty.

Around ten-thirty, I found the house, a hip-roofed Colonial Revival from 1920 or so, not very different from the house my mother had lived in for the last forty years of her life, and less than a mile away from it.

A few minutes after I rang the bell, a man in a robe and carrying a section of the Sunday *New York Times* opened the door. (Aha! They were screening calls. The nerve.)

"Yes?" he said through the screen door.

"I was wondering if I could speak with Lucille Baker," I answered.

He turned away from me and called out, "Lucy, it's for you."

Then he turned back and said, "She'll be here in a minute."

"Thank you." I said, and then, as he continued to stand in the doorway, wondered what other small talk was expected of me and just what a writer working on a *New Yorker* profile might say under the circumstances.

"Lovely weather," I murmured.

"Yes," he said.

I decided that was the extent of my obligation to make conversation; I suspected he didn't much want to talk to me, either, and his continuing presence was to ensure that I didn't walk off with the welcome mat.

Lucy arrived in the promised minute, in a housecoat and slippers. Her resemblance to Tally left me breathless for a moment. The welcome-mat-protector continued to hover in the background.

"Yes?" she said.

"Mrs. Baker, I'm Margaret Connor, and I'm working on a profile for the *New Yorker*. I'd like to talk to you, if I may, about your sister."

"My sister?" she said. "I don't have a sister."

"I'm talking about Paula Chandler," I answered, thinking that my cover story, even with modifications, wasn't going to hold up here very well. "I'm doing a profile on a friend of Paula's who was profoundly affected by her death; it influenced much of her later work."

"Who?" she said.

"Catherine Christiansen," a name I remembered from the same high school yearbook page on which Paula's picture had appeared.

"Never heard of her," Lucy answered.

"She was a high school classmate of Paula's," I said, knowing that at least would check out. "She's going to become very well known if she wins the Pulitzer Prize later this year, but of course right now we're only guessing that she'll win," I struggled on, wondering what I would do if she refused to talk to someone writing about Catherine Christiansen. But once again I benefited from the lure of the *New Yorker;* she decided to talk to me.

"Well, you might as well come in," she said. "Forgive our disarray, but we weren't expecting company," she said pointedly.

"I apologize for just showing up, but I was in the neighborhood and thought I'd take a chance on catching you at home," I said, as she led me into the living room.

I looked around and decided that if there was money on this side of Tally's family, it wasn't being lavished here. The house itself would sell for at least $325 thousand, but most of the people living in this neighborhood couldn't afford the houses they lived in if they hadn't lived there for at least twenty years. The furniture was tasteful but inexpensive and well worn; in fact, it looked about like mine.

"We're just having coffee," Lucy said, "Can I offer you some?" I accepted, since it would give me time to figure out what I was going to ask. I had been so busy thinking about my cover story, it hadn't occurred to me what I was going to try to learn from this interview.

The man, whom I assumed—correctly, as it later turned out—to be Mr. Randolph Baker, settled into what was clearly his chair and resumed his consumption of the Sunday *Times.* I couldn't fault him for that; done properly, reading the Sunday *Times* is a several-hour proposition, and once you fall behind, you never catch up. There is some advantage to regularly reading a newspaper where it doesn't matter a whole lot if you miss a day or two.

Once the coffee was served and Lucy settled across from me, she said, "Now what's this all about?"

In a great show of writerly behavior, I took out a pad and pen to take notes as I began.

"Catherine Christiansen is a major American poet whose work was profoundly affected by your sister's death at such a young age. I'm trying to get some sense of your sister so that I can explain why her death had such a great impact on Catherine." I congratulated myself that at least I had remembered the name I used, but I thought I had probably said "profoundly affected" one more time than was good for me.

"I couldn't tell you anything about that. She was a normal kid—she was five years younger than I am, so I didn't know her high school friends very much, but she seemed to have the normal quota of them. I had already left home; Randy and I were married when I was nineteen. Paula was quite pretty, or at least I always thought so."

I nodded agreement. "I've seen her picture," I said, thinking that she wasn't just pretty, she was beautiful, but I was prejudiced. "You looked a lot alike, didn't you?" I asked, knowing that once Lucy met Tally, she wouldn't have any difficulty in believing who Tally's mother was.

"Yes, I suppose we did, although Paula was smaller than I am—not petite, exactly, but more slender and fragile-looking."

I nodded some more. The less I said, the less likely I was to get myself into trouble. Nodding, fortunately, worked.

"She was a happy person most of the time, the kind of person other people like to be around. Very outgoing and considerate."

Vigorous nodding from me.

"And she was smart, too. If there'd been enough money, she could have gone to a good college easily. As it was, mother had to really scrape to make the Katie Gibbs tuition. We always hoped that, once she got married, she could go back to school."

"Married?" I said. "Was she planning to be married?"

"Oh, no, she wasn't engaged or anything, but in those days you just assumed that that was what you were going to do with your life."

"Was there any particular man in her life?"

"She dated a lot, but I don't think there was anyone in particular, or at least I'm not sure. In those days, it was considered acceptable to play the field—not like today, where the only choices seem to be either group dates or committed relationships. I think there may have been someone for a while, but then she suddenly upped and moved away. I never saw her the last six months of her life. She didn't even come home for Christmas that year; she said she was too busy. Thanksgiving was the last time I saw her."

"Where did she move to?" I asked.

"Upstate somewhere." To Westchesterites, upstate is anything north of the county line, and takes in an immense amount of territory.

"Whereabouts?"

"I was never quite sure; she didn't give me an address because she said she was moving around so much, she'd just stay in touch. She called and I spoke to her every few weeks; I think she was around Albany somewhere."

"Was she living with a man?" I asked, taking a plunge into the deep end.

"Of course not!" she responded indignantly. "Paula was a good girl; nice girls didn't do that in those days."

Oops. I was in trouble now. There didn't seem to be any point in asking about the pregnancy or the baby. I thought to myself of the number of nice girls who did do that in those days but decided it was better to head off in another direction.

"Do you know what she was doing on the Taconic at that hour of the night?"

"No, we never did know that. Maybe that Catherine person knows. Mother thought maybe she was coming home, but there wasn't any luggage in the car. A week or so later, mother got all her things shipped from Albany, but there was no name or return address on the boxes the stuff came in. After the accident, it didn't seem to matter much."

"Did Paula ever go by the nickname 'PJ'?" I asked.

"Some people called her that, or sometimes 'Paula J.' Why do you ask?"

"Some of the materials I'm researching refer to a 'PJ' and I just wanted to be sure that PJ and Paula were one and the same. Do you by any chance know if she had a friend named Susan Franklin?" I asked.

"The name doesn't ring any bells. Was she a friend of that Catherine person, too?"

"No, not necessarily," I said, shaking my head. Of course, it didn't mean that Paula and Susan didn't know each other; still, if she had answered yes, it would have put a much-needed link in the chain.

I took a shot in the dark. "What about Dolly?" I said.

"Yeah, what about Dolly," she echoed sarcastically. "Great good friend Dolly never showed up for the funeral, never called, never did anything. She just disappeared off the face of the earth. Every time I talked to Paula it was 'Dolly this' and 'Dolly that,' as if the sun rose and set on Dolly. Mother said she thought Dolly was living with Paula upstate and she must have been the one who sent the boxes, but we never heard anything from her. I thought it was very damn strange, myself. Not even a telephone call. It wouldn't have been that hard for her to call my poor mother at least.'' Thirty years later Lucy still resented the woman's behavior.

Poor Dolly, I thought to myself—she was too busy saving Tally from whatever threatened her to pass along condolences to the Chandlers. Fortunately, it didn't occur to Lucy to ask me how I knew about Dolly.

"You wouldn't by any chance know Dolly's last name or where she lived, would you?" A long shot, but if the threat didn't come from the Chandler family, and I was fairly certain by now that it didn't, then it came from Tally's father's side, and Dolly was the only connection I had to Tally's father, if I had any at all.

"Rivers," she answered with a dull voice. "Her mother was Maria Rivers, and they lived in an apartment in Mount Vernon. I know because one time Paula asked me to take some things to their apartment so Dolly could pick them up."

I knew I should probably pursue the whereabouts of Paula's "stuff" from Albany, although it was most likely long gone, but I'd lost my taste for the task. This was my last shot, too, because by tomorrow they would know that Catherine Christiansen wasn't a major American poet and I wouldn't be welcome again, or at least not until I had a different story to tell.

I looked pointedly at my watch, exclaimed that this had been so interesting that I had quite forgotten the time and that I was going to be late for another appointment, and skedaddled as quickly as politeness allowed. I could only hope that Lucy Baker would forgive me when she knew the truth that I hoped I could tell her soon.

I drove a few blocks and pulled over to the curb to use the laptop.

I was as convinced as I could be that Paula's family wasn't the source of the problem. There seemed to be no dark secrets here, except of course that Paula had had her baby in secret, keeping it from her family. Considering that it was 1966, that didn't seem so surprising. It did suggest that the father was a married man, despite Lucy's protestations that Paula wasn't that kind of girl. Paula may have been waiting for him to make an honest woman of her, as they said at the time, before she sprang the news on her family. Once a woman had a wedding band on her finger, her earlier transgressions were easier to forgive; matrimony lent such things a certain retrospective respectability.

She might have had quite a wait, as getting a divorce in New York might not have been all that easy, not to mention that some people have been known to promise to get a divorce without actually doing anything about it. I couldn't remember exactly when the divorce laws had changed in New York State, but it was probably some time in the 'sixties. Before the change, adultery was just about the only grounds, and only the injured party could seek the divorce, so getting a divorce from an uncooperative spouse was tricky. Indeed, entrapping the uncooperative spouse in a compromising situation to create grounds for divorce was virtually a business in its own right. The laws might have already been changed by 1966, but divorce was still a major scandal in some circles.

But certainly Tally hadn't been put up for adoption—which would have been another choice in the 'sixties—or at least not in the usual sense of the phrase. Based on Hunter's report of what Peter had done about the birth records, certainly no normal adoption process had been involved. If Dolly had been with Paula at the birth, the one explanation that seemed to fit what I knew was that Dolly had spirited the baby away—probably after the accident—and delivered her into Susan's and Peter's hands.

I needed to know who the father was. And I had nothing.

I popped the lid on the laptop and sent off a quick note to Tally telling her that I had seen her aunt but hadn't yet told her the truth. Then I accessed the phone directory data base.

To quote Celie, "Bingo!"

I couldn't believe my luck—or so it seemed at the time—when it popped up a number and an address for Maria Rivers in Mount Vernon, New York. I hit the "map" button, and got a display of a street map of the area with the block highlighted.

SEVENTEEN

I STOPPED AT the deli in the Wykagyl shopping center in New Rochelle to have a pastrami-and-corned-beef sandwich—not quite in a class with Wolf's in Manhattan, but reliably good for forty years that I knew about. Although you can get pastrami and corned beef in Colorado, they come in sterile plastic wrappers and are sliced into neat dry slices with a slicer and heated in a microwave rather than being forked out of covered tray on a steaming hot table and being cut with a knife and oozing juices all over the countertop.

There's a difference.

Thus fortified, I headed for Mount Vernon.

Mount Vernon was a part of Westchester that I did not know at all, except for the ranks of aging apartment houses glimpsed from the Cross County Parkway in the days when I had regularly made the trip from Manhattan to New Rochelle and back. The map took me to one of these elderly apartment houses, half-timbered in a Tudor style, and probably built in the 'twenties. It had seen better days, but had a certain shabby elegance. The buildings had likely been a smart Westchester address when they were new, and the apartments would be fairly large. I would have put money on the likelihood that they were now co-ops.

Fortunately, I found a parking spot in the shade of a huge old maple only half a block from my destination. I let Molly out for a brief walk and was able to make productive use of Sheila's pooper scooper before

I put her back in the car.

Reluctantly, I slipped the Ferragamos back on. To my mind, Ferragamo and Bruno Magli between them make the most comfortable women's dress shoes possible. However, in my life, the expression "comfortable women's dress shoes" would be an oxymoron if it didn't have too many words in it to qualify. Even the sturdy inch-and-a-quarter heels on these were torture.

The door of the apartment house was at the back of a minuscule courtyard decorated with stone planters with no plants in them. The tiny lobby had a black-and-white tile floor, as I knew it would. I found "M. Rivers" in apartment 3C and pushed the button. A minute later the door buzzed and I entered the hall. The intercom was probably broken. So much for security.

The elevator groaned and creaked its way slowly to the third floor while I considered the possibility that climbing the stairs was occasionally the better idea. But we made it all the way.

The hall smelled in a pleasant way of Sunday cooking, and you could hear muffled voices and TV sounds coming from behind the apartment doors. I rang the bell at 3C and a minute later heard chain locks being fastened and door locks unfastened. The door opened a crack to reveal a woman about my own age, dressed in jeans and a T-shirt, who said, "Yes?" Too young to be Dolly's mother. A sister, maybe.

"Maria Rivers?" I asked.

"Just a minute," she said to me and "Ma, it's for you," to the room behind her.

"Who is it?" I heard.

"I don't know—some lady."

"What's she want?"

"I want to talk to her about Dolly," I answered. My head was now well and truly out of the foxhole.

"Dolly?" she said to me in disbelief. "Hold on," she said and closed the door.

I wasn't quite sure what was going on, so I followed instructions and held on. A minute later, I could hear the chain being unfastened and she opened the door wide and ushered me with a gesture into the living room.

The room was crammed with overstuffed furniture. It was in semi-darkness because the drapes had been drawn, presumably to keep the bright daylight outside from dimming the televised baseball game.

"Johnny, turn that thing down," the woman said to a youngish man sprawled in a lounge chair. He picked up a remote and notched the sound down a little.

An elderly woman appeared in the archway leading from the living room to the spaces beyond and said, "Come into the kitchen where we can talk." I picked my way carefully across the room, trying not to lose any shin to table corners, and followed her a short way down the hall and into the kitchen, where natural daylight was allowed in. The younger woman followed me, and when the elderly woman sat down at the kitchen table and motioned me to do likewise, she took the other seat at the table.

"I'm Maria Rivers," the old woman said. "Did he send you?" Her tone was not friendly at all.

"He?" I said. "I don't think so. I came on my own. I don't know who you're talking about."

"How do you know Dolly?" she asked, still with an icy coldness.

"I'm afraid I don't know Dolly. I know a friend of

hers and when her friend learned that I was going to be in New York, she asked me to look for you." Florrie would hardly mind this slight variation of the truth.

"Why?"

I decided that if I was going to get answers rather than questions, I had to turn this conversation around fairly drastically.

"I'm sorry to have to tell you that Dolly is dead," hoping by everything that's holy that she and I were talking about the same Dolly.

She was visibly shaken by this, but she still wasn't ready to believe that I wasn't the enemy. "How do you know this?"

"I've spoken to her stepdaughter and to her friend and to the policeman who is investigating her death."

"How do you know it was my Dolly?" she asked.

I was guessing, but she didn't need to know that. "I know from her stepdaughter that she called you at eight o'clock on the twenty-seventh of every month for years. If it wasn't your Dolly, how would I know that?"

That hit the mark. She started to cry. The younger woman embraced her and held her as the sobs grew deeper and more wracking.

After what seemed like forever, the sobs gave over to nose-blowing and mopping up a small but steady flow of tears. The younger woman said, "I'll make a fresh pot of coffee," and I knew we were about to get to the business at hand. There are some cultures in which the making of a fresh pot of coffee signals the beginning of serious discussion, and this was clearly one of them.

"How did she die?" the old woman finally asked when she had collected herself enough to speak again.

"I'll tell you everything I can," I said, "but you

need to know first that there is a mystery surrounding her death and I need you to tell me everything you know so that I can find out who's responsible.''

She nodded her assent, as if it was no surprise to her that there was a mystery involved.

"She died of a heart attack in Los Angeles, and the police think someone was questioning her when she died. They're calling it murder.''

Maria crossed herself in a reflexive gesture.

"Los Angeles? Did she live in Los Angeles?''

"No, she was just visiting. She lived in Santa Barbara.''

"Santa Barbara? Where's that?''

"It's about a hundred miles up the coast from Los Angeles. She was a widow and lived with her stepdaughter and her stepdaughter's two children.''

"I knew she had a stepdaughter; she told me that, and about the grandchildren. I didn't know her name, though. What was her name?''

It certainly couldn't hurt anything to let that out now; the people from whom it was supposed to be a secret surely knew. "Miller. Dolly Miller. Her stepdaughter's name is Madelyn Cross, and I know she'd like to talk to you about Dolly. She really loved her. I'll have her call you as soon as we get this matter resolved. Now tell me about Dolly.''

"She was a wonderful daughter. She was a trained nurse, you know,'' she said with pride. I nodded as if I had known—that would explain why she was with Paula; she might even have delivered the baby.

She went on, "She made the down payment on this place when it went co-op. Otherwise Teresa and Johnny and I would have been out on the street.''

"When did she leave?''

"She went upstate in the winter of 'sixty-five, but she wasn't hiding then; she was just working up there. Then, in the summer of 'sixty-six, she suddenly disappeared. I didn't hear from her for weeks and weeks, and then when I did, she would never tell me where she was. Every couple of years she'd show up for a visit, always after dark, and she'd leave before dawn. I never knew when she was coming. But, like you said, she called on the twenty-seventh of every month at eight o'clock. The last time was just a few weeks ago. Now she won't be calling again, ever." And the crying started anew. This time it wound down more quickly, and the pouring of the coffee and the administering of cream and sugar gave us all an opportunity to collect ourselves.

"When I first came in," I said, "you asked if 'he' had sent me. Who were you talking about?"

"The cop," she said.

"What cop?"

"I don't know his name, but he's come looking for Dolly a couple of times a year for the last thirty years. The last time, he was really nasty about it and said if she didn't show up soon, he was going to have to hurt one of us. This time he was asking lots of questions about who she'd worked for before she disappeared."

"When was the last time he was here?"

"On the twenty-fifth. Just two days before Dolly called. When I told her about it, she got very upset and told me I mustn't tell him anything, anything at all."

"Is he in his sixties, about five-ten, maybe two hundred pounds, bald, and kind of grayish-looking?" I asked, feeding back what I remembered of the description given by the desk clerk at the San Carlos.

Maria nodded and Teresa nodded along with her.

"Does the San Carlos Court mean anything to you?"

They nodded again. "It's where we all stayed the one time we made a trip to California when the girls were young and before their Daddy died. There's still a postcard on the mantelpiece from that trip. Get the postcard, Teresa." Teresa responded quickly, apparently not wanting to miss any of the conversation. It was indeed a postcard of a considerably smaller San Carlos Court, taken some half century earlier. Even though it had faded, you could tell that it had once been garishly colored in the postcard-art style of the day.

"I'm afraid I have to tell you that this is where Dolly died."

The tears started anew, this time with Teresa leading the way. I suspect the memories of her childhood trip with her sister affected her more than anything else we'd talked about so far. Again we had to wait until the crying subsided. I couldn't remember ever having felt so drained.

"Have you ever heard of Paula Chandler?"

Maria nodded. "That's who Dolly was working for when she went upstate. I remember Paula had a cute little red sports car. I never heard what became of her."

"She was killed in an accident in that sports car," I said. "How about Susan Franklin?"

"She worked for some family named Franklin when she first got her license," Maria said. "I don't remember whether there was anyone named Susan."

"In Larchmont?"

"Yes. It was somewhere up there. She took the New York, New Haven and Hartford to get there, I know." Somehow "Amtrak" lacks the cadence and stylishness of "The New York, New Haven and Hartford," not that the NY, NH & H had any actual style except in its name.

"What else can you tell me about the cop?" I asked.

They looked at each other and shrugged.

"Well, if you think of anything else, or if he shows up again, I need to know as soon as possible. Here's my number at the hotel where I'm staying, and the extension; let me write it down for you."

When I was finally out on the street again, after many teary hugs and pats from the Rivers women, I was shocked to see that I had only been there a little over two hours; it had seemed forever.

I shed the Ferragamos for my clogs and took Molly for a little walk in the tiny park across from the apartment house. Somehow, the old cop had gotten from the Rivers enough to send him to the San Carlos Court. What it could possibly have been, I had no idea, nor did I know how he had recognized Dolly when he saw her. On the other hand, if he knew at all what she looked like—and maybe, like Paula and Lucy and Tally, there was a strong family resemblance between Maria and Dolly, or, even more likely, Teresa and Dolly—and he was expecting to find her there, it might not have been difficult to recognize her.

As I came back to the car, I saw Johnny, who I conjectured was Teresa's son, walking down the other side of the street, headed for the corner, but I didn't think anything of it. I almost called out to him to ask if he knew anything additional about the old cop, but I was really too tired to spend more time talking to a Rivers today. I got in the car and Molly and I headed back up the Hutchinson River Parkway to the hotel.

EIGHTEEN

BACK IN THE HOTEL, I indulged myself in a long soak in the bathtub. My house in Colorado is equipped with a bathtub designed for bathing children under the age of ten, so while I usually prefer a shower, the occasional luxury of a soak in a generously-proportioned bathtub is not to be taken lightly.

After that I changed into a set of sweats that had just come back from the hotel laundry. I was amused to see that they had seen fit to iron a crease in the pants—these sweats had never looked so good before.

I then spent at least an hour on the phone with Tally and the Snowdens, who evidently were planning to stay in Palo Alto for as long as they thought it necessary to protect Tally. I thought of Florrie's girls and decided that wasn't a bad idea at all. If my "old cop" was going to show up on her doorstep, he'd get a different reception than he found at the Rivers apartment.

I toyed with the idea of calling Bruce Morita and filling him in, but it was Sunday and he wouldn't be in his office, and I didn't feel much like trying to explain my message to a stranger. Tomorrow would be time enough.

My stomach told me that it had been a long time since the deli in New Rochelle, so I called room service and ordered a three-course dinner and a half bottle of wine, along with a hamburger patty for Molly, because I didn't feel like sharing my grilled salmon with her.

That done, I flipped on the laptop and dialed up

through Palo Alto to my Internet service provider so I
could read my mail and catch up with my newsgroups.
In one of them, I was in the midst of our bimonthly
flaming debate about the use of the singular "they" in
preference to such barbarisms as "he or she," "he/
she," or, even worse, "s/he."

I was fully engrossed in preparing one of my more
scintillating responses to some dimwit when there came
a knock on the door. It was too soon for it to be room
service with our dinners, so I peeked through the fish-
eye in the door. My heart sank. I didn't want to open
the door to the two-hundred-pound, five-ten, grayish-
looking hat-in-hand bald man in the hall, but if I didn't
I'd miss any chance to find out who he was. I backed
off from the door and picked up Molly and threw her
in the bathroom.

Then I called out, "Just a minute," and looked about
the room frantically for some means of protection. All
I saw was the open laptop, and I suddenly remembered
Steve saying "and this is the panic button." I couldn't
remember exactly what he had said it would do, but it
was something about transmitting sound back to Palo
Alto. I clicked on it. A message flashed briefly, but I
didn't see what it said, and the screen went dark.
Gently, I closed the lid.

I went back to the door and said, "Who is it?"

"Mrs. Rivers sent me; I have some information for
you," he answered. I put the chain on, and opened the
door, knowing as I did so that the chain was no protection at all to someone determined to come in.

"I can't tell you standing out here in the hall like
this," he said in stagy whisper. Against every ounce
of judgment I have ever had in my life, I closed the
door to release the chain and opened it to admit him.

I motioned him to a chair on one side of the desk that held my mute laptop. I wasn't even sure it was still on; in its normal state, it was utterly silent when running flat out, and it lacked the usual idiot lights so there was no way to tell.

"Who are you?" I said, hoping against all expectation that I would get some revealing information.

"Just an old friend of Maria Rivers," he said.

"What does she have for me?" I asked, pretending to believe his story.

Just then Molly jumped at the bathroom door in protest; there was a visitor to investigate.

"What's that?"

"It's my dog. I put her in the bathroom."

"I don't mind dogs—you can let her out."

"No, she's not good with strangers," I said, wantonly slandering her character.

"What kind of a dog is she?"

"A Westie."

"One of those little white ones?"

"Yes."

"Shit," he said. "You're the broad who came to the house in a cab in Santa Barbara." He lifted his hand from where it had been out of sight and rested it on the desk. It had a large, ugly gun in it. I decided that the time for innocence was over and it was now time to brazen it out.

"While you were waiting for a chance to ransack it," I answered.

"Yeah. But there were too many people around that day. I woulda been seen. I went back and got it later."

"And you're the man who killed Dolly Miller," I went on, jumping in with both feet.

"I didn't kill her. She just croaked."

"The police are calling it murder," I answered.

"Tough. They'll never make it stick. But I don't want to talk about that, I want to talk about the kid."

"What kid?"

"The kid that Dolly Rivers, Miller, Buchner—whatever her name was—took from Rhinebeck in nineteen sixty-six."

"Rhinebeck?" I couldn't help but saying. Not Albany, but about halfway there. Is that where Paula and Dolly had been holed up?

"Rhinebeck. By the time I got there, everything was gone."

"First tell me who the father is and then I'll tell you where the kid is," I said recklessly. After letting slip that "Rhinebeck," there didn't seem to be any point in continuing the fiction that I didn't know what he was talking about.

"Lady, I don't have to tell you a damn thing. I'm the one asking the questions."

"But it's the father who's important, isn't it?"

"The father is just as dead as the mother. They saw to that," he answered.

"Who saw to it?"

"You still don't get it, do you—I'm the one with the gun."

Voicing a courage I did not feel, I said, "I'm not telling you anything."

He rose out of his chair and leaned towards me. "Then I'll find out for myself, and when I do, it's bye-bye girlie for both of you." I realized what he was doing too late to react to it—he hit the side of my head with the hand that held the gun.

I came to and found myself lying where I had fallen from the chair, except that my hands were tied painfully behind my back with what was probably the drapery pull cord. He was standing right in front of my face and going through the files in my attaché case.

He kept muttering foul expletives to himself as he went through the clippings that Celie had printed for me. Fortunately, those and a copy of the page from Paula's yearbook were the only papers I had; there was nothing anywhere about Tally. Anything relating to Tally or FR&R, such as my expense records, was on the system in Palo Alto, and even if he had the knowledge to look at what was on the laptop, he wouldn't find anything.

At one point, he looked down at me and I quickly closed my eyes, hoping he wouldn't realize I was awake. I wasn't anxious to have his attention. He said, "Sure you don't know who the father was, bitch. Who do you think you're kidding?" I couldn't figure out what that might mean.

He moved on from my attaché case to my handbag. "Boulder, Colorado?" I heard him say to himself. "What the shit does Boulder, Colorado, have to do with anything?"

After a few more minutes, he prodded me ungently in the rib cage with the toe of his shoe.

"You awake, bitch?"

I groaned, which came naturally enough under the circumstances. He sat me up unceremoniously, leaning me against the end of the bed.

"If you tell me where the kid is, I'll let you go," he said.

"I don't believe that for a minute. You'll never let me go knowing what I know."

"Nobody can say I didn't give you a chance."

"They're going to catch you, you know. They'll find you. After all, I found you."

"You didn't find me. I found you," he said.

"Yeah, but they'll sweat Maria Rivers's grandson—that kid down in Mount Vernon—until he gives you up," I answered, guessing that it was Johnny who'd fingered me. And, in the remote possibility that this conversation was being transmitted to Palo Alto, I wanted to make sure they knew to talk to Johnny when I couldn't tell them any more.

"They can try, but he won't be telling them much of anything."

"He knows how to get in touch with you, and LAPD knows why I'm here."

"Like I said, they can try."

"Besides, you can only do so much mayhem to old ladies in hotel rooms before they get on to you."

"That's why it's not going to be here," he said. "You're going to have a little accident—there's a sweet little place on the service road on the backside of this hill that'll do just fine. I won't even have far to walk to get back to my car. They probably won't find you for a week. Get up." He prodded me even harder with his shoe. Kicked wouldn't have been an inappropriate description. It was sore enough that I suspected he had already worked on me several times while I was unconscious.

"I can't." I said. This, at least, was true enough. While I really didn't want to be splattered all over a hotel room floor, I wasn't physically capable of getting myself up with my hands tied. I didn't want to be splattered all over a Westchester hillside, either, but that was at least several minutes in the future, and anything could happen in those minutes.

Not happily, and with great effort, he got me to my feet. Needless to say, he made several unflattering remarks about my girth in the process. I was somewhat cooperative, because he had the gun in one hand the whole time he was doing it and he could still exercise the option of shooting me on the spot. He grabbed my car keys from the pile of stuff he'd dumped on the desk when he went through my handbag.

"If you leave that purse, they'll know I didn't go voluntarily," I said. I figured the more encumbered he was, the easier it might be for me to find a way to upset his applecart. He picked up the inverted handbag and stuffed most of its contents back in with one hand while he held me and the gun with the other.

That done, he picked up the bag, looped the strap around my neck, and marched me across the room to the door. All I had succeeded in doing was getting myself encumbered.

He pinned me facing the wall with his forearm, while he checked to see if the hall was clear. Unhappily for me, it was. Not even room service with my dinner. At the end of the corridor was a door to the back parking lot; he marched me to it.

"Where's your car?" he barked in my ear.

"On the lower level; it's the white Taurus down at the end there." The back parking lot was on two levels, connected by a cement staircase with about six steps. As we were starting toward it, a couple came out of the hotel behind us. He whirled me around to face him, shoved me up against the nearest car, and pretended to be kissing me as they passed. I could feel the gun pressing against my ribs at the same time as he pressed his body hard against mine to keep me from moving. He stank of stale cigarettes and alcohol. I responded to this unwelcome attention by violently throwing up the moment he released me. "Bitch," he muttered over

and over again, trying unsuccessfully to stay clear of
the stream of vomit without letting go of me. Unfortunately, this went unobserved by the couple, who were
already pulling out of the lot by the time I could raise
my head again.

I felt my knees starting to give. Whatever shreds of
bravado had kept me going this far were deserting me.
I wanted to stop and cry, and I wanted to go to the
bathroom, and I wanted to take a shower, and I wanted
my mother, and none of that was going to happen as
he pushed me in front of him toward the top of the
stairs, prodding me with the gun whenever I showed
any reluctance.

We had just reached the top of the stairs when the
cavalry arrived, in the form of four police cruisers.
There were two of them at each end of the lot; they
had appeared out of nowhere with sirens blaring and
lights blazing. With one at each end of the upper lot
and one at each end of the lower lot, we were effec-
tively encircled. We stopped in our tracks.

They cut their sirens, but left the multicolored lights
whirling. It was the most beautiful sight I had ever
seen. The four patrol cars produced eight policemen
with guns drawn and ready. Somebody, somewhere,
had a great deal of clout. I thanked my unknown ben-
efactor, but then I realized I still had a big ugly gun
stuck in my ribs.

He let loose his grip on my arms to instead grab me
around the neck, and, holding the gun to my head, used
me as a shield and hostage.

"It's all over," one of the policemen shouted. "Let
her go."

I don't know what possessed me at that point, except
the certain knowledge that my weight had to be an

advantage here, and I wanted to make him reconsider his remarks about it. Gathering all my resources, I began to push back against him, thinking I could possibly make him stagger and fall before he had the wits to shoot me in the head.

"Bitch," he said once again as he shifted his grip to behind my shoulders and pitched me forward down the cement staircase. With my hands tied behind me, I could do nothing to break my fall; I might as well have been a sack of potatoes for all the control I had over the situation. As I was falling, I heard a loud explosion and then I was falling and tumbling and falling some more and then the lights went out again.

NINETEEN

THE NEXT THING I knew, I was lying somewhere flat on my back. I worked my eyes open to see a man in a white coat hanging a new bag on a saline drip, so I knew I was getting medical attention for something.

The man in the white coat smiled at me and said, "Hey, look who just joined us. Hello."

"Am I shot?" I managed to croak through a dry mouth.

"No. You're pretty banged up, but not shot. The good news is that there isn't anything that time won't heal. The bad news is that everything is going to hurt like hell for several days." He held up a water bottle and, with a gesture and a look, asked if I wanted some. When I nodded, he stuck the straw in my mouth. I was fairly certain my own hands were somewhere about, but I hadn't gotten to the point of finding them yet, so I was grateful not to have to use them.

After I'd had a couple of good slugs of water, I asked, "Molly?"

Someone wearing a dark blue uniform moved into my line of vision.

"Officer Stephens, White Plains Police, Ms. Connor," he said. "I have two messages that I'm supposed to give you as soon as you wake up. First, Molly is being well taken care of."

"Thank you," I croaked.

"Second, Detective Morita of the Los Angeles Police Department sends his compliments and thanks you for catching his murderer for him.''

"So they caught him?'' I asked.

"There was an exchange of gunfire and he was killed at the scene, just after he threw you down the stairs,'' he replied.

"Omigod,'' I said, "was anyone else hurt?''

"No, there were no other casualties.''

"Where am I?''

"You're in the White Plains Medical Center Emergency Room; we're about to admit you to the hospital,'' the doctor answered.

"And we'll be keeping a twenty-four-hour watch on you to make sure no one else tries to get to you,'' Officer Stephens added.

I nodded like this made sense, but it didn't. Then I turned back to the doctor and said, "Am I on morphine?''

"Dilaudid. Is it working?''

"I guess so; I don't feel much of anything.''

"Count your blessings; you will soon enough.''

"My glasses?''

"We have them; they weren't broken, but you don't need them now.''

All the really major things seemed to be accounted for, and my brain steadfastly refused to go on thinking any more.

"Should I go to sleep now?''

"That's probably a pretty good idea.''

I SORT OF half-woke when they took me from the ER cubicle to a hospital room, but the next time I was fully aware of my surroundings, there was new daylight in the room and Charlie was sitting in a chair reading. As soon as he saw me move, he got up and brought me the water bottle—so that I guessed that he'd had experience with drugs and knew that thirty seconds without water was torture.

"Hi," I managed, after I had sucked greedily at the straw.

"Hi," he answered, gently lifting a lock of hair off my face.

"Do you have Molly?" I asked.

"Yes, and she already has Martha, my housekeeper, and her husband Mike, who drove us the other night, completely trained, not to mention me."

"How did the police know to come?"

"I'm not sure; it had something to do with the computer. They said you hit the panic button and it set off all sorts of alarms in Palo Alto. They were monitoring everything that happened in the room, and as soon as they realized there was a threat to you, they called the police. After things were under control, Hunter called me. Of course, I got Molly right away. Tally was beside herself until she knew that both of you were all right. How do you feel now?"

"Very sore all over, and my head is splitting. Am I all right?"

"You were concussed, among other things. He hit you on the head in the hotel room, they think, and then you hit it a couple more times falling down the stairs. You've been in and out of consciousness ever since. That's probably the worst of it, but you banged things up really good. You're going to find stitches in lots of places and bruises all over—one side of you is completely black and blue, they tell me. But they assure me there is no lasting damage."

"Who was he?"

"His name was Jack Sheeley, and he was a private investigator."

"A private eye?" I tried to figure out how that made sense, but I couldn't. "Has anyone talked to Maria Rivers's grandson?" I asked.

"Not yet. Tally pieced together what you'd told her on the phone earlier with what Sheeley said in the hotel room and told the police who to look for, but the Mount Vernon police reported that he was missing—had been since last night."

"Oh, Charlie, you don't think…"

"His mother said it wasn't unusual for him to go out for several days and show up again when he needed clean clothes or more money, so he'll probably turn up yet."

"What happened in the parking lot? They told me he was shot in an exchange of gunfire, but how did it happen?"

"The way the scene was described to me, you were well on your way to knocking him off his feet when he pushed you away to prevent it. Once he didn't have you as a shield, they would have him nailed. He opened fire."

"But that was suicidal. There were too many of them. Why didn't he just surrender?"

"We'll probably never know the answer to that one, but that isn't an entirely unknown form of suicide, either."

"It has to be Johnny who fingered me. I simply can't imagine Maria or Teresa doing that, and Lucy and Randy Baker don't know who I really am or where I'm staying. I wish they would find Johnny. Then we could find out if I'm right in thinking he told Sheeley where to find Dolly, as well."

"Don't worry about it now; they're looking for him. You still need mostly to sleep. Got to knit up that raveled sleeve."

In a manner uncharacteristic of every private eye in every novel I had ever read—PIs are, to a man, disregardful of medical advice in order to undertake the hot pursuit of the bad guys at the earliest possible opportunity—I turned over and went back to sleep. Frankly, I don't recall that my body gave me that much choice in the matter.

The next time I woke, it was to find a strange but thoroughly pleasant and cheerful looking middle-aged woman in my room. She, too, brought me the water bottle as soon as she noticed I was awake.

"I'm Martha, the judge's housekeeper," she said to my unasked question. "The judge said you wouldn't care for the hospital food, so I brought you lunch. I also brought you a change of clothes and a robe from your hotel room. The clothes you were wearing were cut off you, I'm afraid. I packed the rest of your things and they're at the judge's house. And I wanted to be sure to tell you that Molly is doing just fine. I would have smuggled her in so you could see for yourself, but the judge said that you would believe me."

I gave her a big smile at that, which was to be the beginning of a great friendship.

"They want you to get up and move around for a while now; you've been lying down too long. The nurse said she'd come when you're ready to remove the drip so you can go for a walk." She left the room. I still hadn't said anything, but there had been nothing necessary to say. I love being fussed over.

She came back with a nurse, who gently but efficiently got me on my feet and enrobed for the ritual parade up and down the hall.

"When can I get out of here?" I asked the nurse, knowing what the answer would be.

"You'll have to ask your doctor that," she said.

"Who's my doctor?" She consulted the chart and said "Doctor Evans—he'll be back in the early evening to talk to you. Can you walk by yourself?"

"I think so," I said, and Martha said, "Don't worry, I'll walk with you in case you need support."

"And bring the water bottle," I said. Martha lifted it high—she already had it in her hand. I adored this woman.

Thanks to the Dilaudid that was still in my system, I had only occasional twinges of the pains that were lurking in the shadows and was able to walk far enough to convince the nurse of my sincere interest in recovery. Each time I passed my guardian in blue, seated just outside my door, we saluted each other. There were a few other patients about doing the hall shuffle along with me, and a few visitors sitting by the nurse's station, but it was a fairly quiet hall.

After eating the lunch that Martha had brought—a steaming corn chowder followed by an enormous salad with all sorts of goodies in it—I went back to sleep.

SOMETIME DURING the afternoon, a detective showed up and interviewed me, but he seemed to know more than I did about what had happened and it didn't take very long to get my statement down.

The next time I woke, it was to late afternoon light and Sheila in my room.

"Hi, baby," I said.

She came to my side and kissed me on the cheek. "It's just not safe to let you out by yourself, is it," she said. "Imagine getting into that much trouble in Westchester County."

"How'd you get here?" I asked.

"Judge Seabrook came down to get me. He insisted, and he said his driver, Mike, will take me home, too," she said.

"Do you just hop in strangers' cars when they invite you?" I asked.

"No, the Judge was pretty smart about that—he had Tally call me first, so I'd know it was safe to go with him. And he wanted Tally to tell me what happened because he didn't want me going nuts when I saw the papers. You made the second section, you know," she said, flashing a headline at me that read COLORADO WOMAN ASSAULTED IN WESTCHESTER HOTEL.

"Just the second section?"

"Don't worry—when the whole truth comes out, you'll make the front page."

"If we ever figure out the whole truth," I said ruefully. "I'm really not any closer than I was when I got here."

"But you've identified Tally's mother, haven't you?"

"Yes, and found her aunt, and identified Dolly Miller, but I still haven't figured out where the threat is coming from."

"Besides Jack Sheeley."

"Right, besides Jack Sheeley. It can't just end with him; that wouldn't make any sense at all. Where is Charlie?" I asked, realizing that, although I kept receiving the benefits of his ministrations, I hadn't seen the man himself since early that morning.

"Right now he's meeting with the DA. They're trying to decide how to proceed without any further risk to you or Tally. In particular, they want to figure out what to release to the press. The press knows there's a police guard on your door and they're very curious as to why."

"So am I for that matter," I said.

"It's pretty obvious, I should think," she said. "No one thinks that Sheeley was acting on his own. There have to be other people involved."

That was certainly true enough.

"But if there are other people involved, they're not going to be influenced by a newspaper report."

"The judge thinks that if we're careful not to show that we know what Sheeley was up to, it may keep them from trying to attack you again. We want them to think you're harmless."

"So far I am harmless."

"I don't know about that; if I were them, I wouldn't want you looking for me. Look at how much you've found out already."

I liked her confidence, even if I didn't share it.

"I told Tally we'd call her as soon as you were ready to talk. Do you want to do that now?"

"After I've been to the potty."

When I started to move to get up, every muscle and organ in my body began to protest.

"You look like you're ready for another shot," Sheila observed. "I'll tell the nurse. The last time she looked in, she said you could have one whenever you wanted."

After I was resettled in bed and shot full of demerol this time, we called Palo Alto.

"You and Hunter saved my life," I said to Tally.

"Your life wouldn't have been in danger if it hadn't been for me," she replied.

"What happened, anyway? I didn't know for sure what the panic button would do."

"The panic button—which, by the way, has never had a live test before—starts up the audio monitor and sets off audible alarms. In your case, it was set to cause alarms both at FR&R and here in my house, as well as my pager, but it was Steve who actually got onto it first at the office, although I was on it here at home only a few seconds later. We heard almost the whole thing, and we have the whole thing captured up until you left the room, of course. Steve came on when you were talking about the dog in the bathroom and I picked up just when you were talking about Rhinebeck. Where is Rhinebeck, anyway?

"Dutchess County, maybe another forty or fifty miles from here, on this side of the river."

"Up the Taconic?"

"Yes, up the Taconic."

"So that's where she was coming from."

"It seems likely."

"Anyway, while I was listening to you guys, Hunter was on the phone to the police back there. I'm not sure exactly what he did to get their attention so fast, but it worked. What was going on in that long period where you didn't say anything? I was scared to death—I thought you might be dead. I was never so relieved as when you spoke again."

"He cold-cocked me."

"What was he doing? He kept muttering all the time."

"Going through my papers. I had all those clippings

that Celie Johnson printed for me, and he was looking at those."

"After you left the room, we just had to wait until Hunter could get hold of someone who could tell him what happened. I was frantic."

"Not to put too fine a point on it, he pushed me down a cement staircase and then was killed in a shoot-out in the parking lot. But not until after I threw up all over him."

"I'm glad to hear that. He was a marked man."

"Indeed he was. He probably reeked to high heaven."

After convincing her that I was going to be okay and telling her no way was she to come east—she was still in danger and I was being well taken care of—we ended the conversation with my promise to personally introduce her to her Aunt Lucy and to Maria Rivers when the time came. Neither of us mentioned what Sheeley had said about her father; there didn't seem to be any point in it.

A severe-looking young man knocked and came in. "I'm Doctor Evans," he introduced himself and I decided immediately that he was going to be no barrel of laughs.

"What kind of a doctor are you?" I asked.

"A neurological surgeon," he answered, as he shined a light into my pupils and waved a finger back and forth for me to follow.

I decided against any remarks about "brain surgery for fun and profit," and said instead, "I trust you haven't scheduled an OR."

"Not yet. We do want to keep you another twenty-four hours because of the number of insults the brain took. We'll run another battery of tests later this evening and again tomorrow afternoon and if you pass those, you're out of here. There are some minor signs of swelling that we want to keep an eye on; if they don't worsen by this time tomorrow, we'll thank your lucky stars and let you go. Of course, you have stitches and bruises all over, but all they should cause you from now on is discomfort.''

"How can you tell there's swelling?"

"We gave you a number of tests that you don't remember. If you weren't unconscious, you were so doped up that you might as well have been. You'll probably remember a little of it in another day or so.'' It occurred to me then that that might explain some of the weird dreams of the past twenty-four hours.

"You mean you were the stranger in my strange dreams?"

"One of them; those of us who weren't stitching you were poking and prodding at you.''

Sheila spoke up, ''Is there anything she can't eat?''

"Nothing except alcohol," he answered.

"Good," she said, "because Judge Seabrook is having dinner brought in for us. He said he had a dinner date with you and he wasn't going to let a little thing like a concussion stand in his way.''

"In that case, can I take a shower? I feel really grotty.''

"Yes, if we cover up your stitches; I'll have a nurse come and give you a hand.''

The shower did as much for me psychologically as it did physically; I must have stood in the spray for fifteen minutes, ridding myself of the memory of the stink of Jack Sheeley. When I finally felt sufficiently clean, Sheila blew dry my hair while the nurse's aid put fresh linens on the bed.

I finally took a complete inventory of the stitching and other mayhem. There were two minor cuts on my face plus an abrasion on one cheek, and I had two absolutely spectacular black eyes and a massive bruise on the side of my face where Sheeley had hit me. Four cuts and numerous abrasions on my arms, three cuts and more abrasions on my legs. The side where Sheeley had been prodding me with his toe was solid black and blue; he'd obviously checked a lot of times to see if I was awake.

"I can't figure out how you got away with no broken ribs," Sheila said.

"Padding," I answered.

Once again, I joined the hall shuffle. Although I felt I was walking a little more confidently than I had earlier, Sheila asked me why I was so contorted and I realized I was favoring my bruised side. Straightening up was agony. Getting over this wasn't going to be any fun at all.

Charlie arrived at six o'clock, just in time to turn away the hospital dinner of chicken noodle soup, mystery meat, instant mashed potatoes, canned peas, iceberg lettuce with bottled Thousand Island dressing, and green gelatin with a dab of ersatz whipped cream. In its place, he ushered in a handsome young waiter with a gorgeous Italian meal—mussels in a mustard-wine sauce, salad of mixed baby greens with a gorgonzola-walnut dressing, spinach-ricotta gnocchi on a bed of baby spinach, breast of chicken saltimbocca with a wild-mushroom risotto, and a strictly American chocolate-hazelnut torte drizzled with creme anglaise and raspberry puree.

Somewhere during the rapturous consumption of all

this, I mentioned that I had to call the hotel and let them know I was returning the next evening.

"No, you're coming to stay with me," Charlie said.

I began to protest, when Sheila said, "Don't be tiresome, Lexy. If you go back to the hotel, I would have to come up here and stay with you and that would be terribly inconvenient for me. Can't you just see, he's dying to have you as his house guest. Let him. That much exposure might help him get over you faster; as it is, he's absolutely ridiculous."

In the face of such wisdom and clarity, I caved immediately.

In any event, it was as merry as a party could be, considering that it hurt when I laughed. It hurt when I didn't laugh, too, so there wasn't much point in avoiding laughter.

The results of my tests that evening were reported to me as "certainly no worse, and maybe even a tiny bit better; have a good night's sleep," and so, with a little help from the hospital pharmacy, I did.

TWENTY

THE NEXT MORNING, Charlie dropped in to bring me up to date.

"I have some news you're not going to like," he said.

"Okay, let me have it."

"A teenage couple looking for some privacy found the body of Johnny Dorset, Maria Rivers's grandson, in the forest alongside Kensico Reservoir late yesterday. He was shot through the back of the head with the same gun Sheeley pulled on you, and hair and fiber evidence puts him in the trunk of Sheeley's car."

I think my voice must have shook as I said, "I killed him. If I hadn't been running around poking into things without knowing what I was doing, he wouldn't have been killed."

"No, no, you mustn't think that. What killed Johnny was his own greed, pure and simple. After you left, he went to the newsstand on the corner and apparently called Sheeley. While he was waiting for Sheeley to show up, he boasted to his friends that he was about to make a big score that would set him up. He evidently thought he could blackmail Sheeley and get away with it. For crying out loud, he knew the guy had killed his aunt, and the only thing that concerned him was what angle he could work on that. Greed and stupidity. That's all it was. He knew he was dealing with a killer."

"And so when Sheeley decided to shoot it out, it

was because he knew they would find Johnny's body sooner or later and pin it on him. What happened to me was no longer relevant.''

"I hadn't thought of that, but it's likely. He would have been looking at murder one for that.''

When I had time to think about it later, I realized that I had been a lot closer that night to joining Johnny than even I thought. I was certainly frightened enough, but I don't think I really believed that I would die on that hillside—that someone could just decide to take my life and do it. But he had done it to Johnny, and he certainly wasn't going to have any compunction about doing it to me. This was definitely outside my experience.

In my head, I knew Johnny's death wasn't my fault, but my heart also knew that it would haunt me for a long time—not for Johnny, perhaps, but for Teresa and Maria, who already had a heavy burden of grief to bear.

I quizzed Charlie about the Sheeley investigation. Sheeley had apparently run a legitimate private investigation operation, except that the majority of his clients didn't account for more than about ten percent of his time, but there were massive billings for "security services" that were paid out of a single numbered account in the Cayman Islands.

"That's who was paying him to find Tally," I said.

"That, or blackmail. Someone was paying him extremely well for something. He owned a townhouse in Hartsdale free and clear and had a really comfortable bank balance, as well.''

"Can they find out who was paying him?''

"Probably not. It takes a lot of arm-twisting to get that information unless you find somebody to bribe, and, for now, the DA's office doesn't seem too eager to take it on.''

"For now?"

"Well, it's not a terribly high priority for them. As far as they're concerned, for all the crimes that were committed—the murder in LA, Johnny's killing, and the assault on you, kidnapping, and attempted murder—the perp is down in the county morgue. So there's not too much percentage for them in going further. They're only doing it now to keep me happy. If they don't turn up something really interesting, and very soon, that would give them a handle on a conspiracy charge of some sort, they're going to give it up."

They had a search warrant for Sheeley's home, which included his office, and Charlie was going along to "observe," so he left again.

Reluctantly, I placed a call to Mount Vernon. I had no idea what reception I might get under the circumstances. Someone whose voice I didn't recognize answered the phone, but eventually Maria came on the line. "I'm so sorry," I said. "I feel responsible."

"You're not responsible," she answered. "He helped the man who killed his Aunt Dolly; he almost got you killed, too. I am ashamed he is my family. So is Teresa."

MY NEXT VISITOR was a real surprise; I had completely forgotten that I had my own private investigator on the case until Sophie Hirsch knocked and came in my room.

"I've been hearing about you," she said, as she closed the door behind her.

"I'll bet," I answered.

"How are you doing?"

"Nothing, they tell me, that time won't cure. How about you?"

"I'm doing good, I think. I have the accident report you wanted," she said, as she pulled a file from her briefcase, "and, under the circumstances, I took the liberty of reading it myself. I think you'll find at least one aspect of it very interesting."

She opened the file folder in front of me and pointed to a box at the top of the first page, where it said "Investigating Officers." The first name of the two in the box was "John H. Sheeley."

"A coincidence?" I asked.

"Not a coincidence. I checked, because I thought you'd want me to," she answered. "Your very own Jack Sheeley, who was at the time a member of the State Highway Patrol and the first officer on the scene."

"So he *was* an old cop. Ever since I first heard of him in Los Angeles, I've thought of him as 'the old cop.' Did you know him? Like, do you have Private Eye dinner-dances or anything like that?"

She laughed heartily at that. "No, I never ran into him, and I do run into most of them around the courthouse. I don't think he worked much around here."

"So it would seem. He got paid a lot of money out of the Cayman Islands."

"Sounds like a good gig. I could use some like that. I do happen to know the other investigating officer, Frank Geoghegan. He was a cop here in White Plains until just recently. He's a real decent guy. I took the liberty of asking him to come by here today because I thought you might like to talk to him."

"Well, I guess I would, now that I think of it," I said.

"He's outside talking to the officer who's guarding you; let me get him." She crossed to the door and stuck her head out. I couldn't hear what was said, but in a minute, the door was opened to admit an immensely tall and jovial Irishman of middle years. Sophie introduced us.

"It's a pleasure, ma'am, but I'm sorry to see you in such a state. Miss Hirsch wouldn't tell me what this was about, but I've been reading in the papers about your run-in with Jack Sheeley."

"Was he a friend of yours?" I asked, thinking that I would have to go carefully if I was talking to one of Sheeley's bosom buddies.

"No. I hardly knew him and it's safe to say that I didn't like what I knew. I thought the manner of his death vindicated my judgment, too. Now, what can I do for you?"

"I really appreciate your coming. Somehow this whole thing ties into a fatal accident that occurred on the Taconic Parkway over thirty years ago. You probably don't even remember it, but you were the second officer on the scene. This is the report," and I turned the file folder and handed it to him so he could look at it. "I haven't read it myself yet," I went on. "Sophie just brought it to me. But we were hoping that you might remember if there was anything unusual about it. The young woman who was killed in that accident is a key figure in the whole mystery surrounding why Jack Sheeley attacked me."

He sat down, took out his glasses, and studied the report for a few minutes.

"I remember this one," he finally said, shaking his head. "It was one of my first ones, and I puked my guts out. God, what a mess it was. It bothered me for a long time."

"What bothered you?"

"Well, that I hadn't been able to keep my cool, for one thing. But I had to get through a lot more of them before I stopped having that reaction, I'm afraid. That was one of the reasons I left the highway patrol to work in White Plains. Fewer smashed-up people."

"Was there anything else?"

"A couple of things. Jack said the guy obviously fell asleep at the wheel, and I didn't know any better at the time, but after I'd seen a bunch more accidents, I began to think that there might have been more to it than that."

"Why?"

"It looked like the big car had actually rammed the little one and pushed it down the slope and into the tree. You know, full on—not the glancing off the fender you expect to find from a car just wandering out of its lane."

"You mean it was deliberate?"

"I wouldn't like to go so far as to say that; I suppose it could have happened accidentally, and of course we're never going to know what actually happened because they're both dead."

"This isn't a courtroom. What do you think happened?"

"I think he rammed her."

"What did Sheeley say?

"Sheeley said, since they were both dead, it really didn't matter how it happened, but maybe she cut him off or something and pissed him off and he was getting even and lost control or something. Of course, nowadays, they just pull a gun and shoot you if you annoy them. Sheeley said it was tragic enough for both families and to conjecture something like a deliberate act could only make it worse for them, and what was the point?"

I laughed involuntarily at the notion of Sheeley being concerned about family sensibilities.

"Sheeley said the insurance companies would settle it, and since the man was pretty clearly at fault, regardless of whether he had the intent or not, her family would get the payout."

"Is there anything else?"

"Yes, there was something else about that one that I didn't realize until I had seen a lot more accidents."

"What?"

"There was no blood in the second car."

"I thought he was thrown clear."

"They were both thrown clear, but her car was still full of blood. If he'd been wearing a seat belt, he could have walked away. I don't think a seat belt could have saved her, though. There probably wasn't one in the Alfa in any case, but the Mercedes might have had one. The Mercedes was wrecked, but the Alfa was eradicated."

"Would there necessarily have been blood in his car?"

"Not necessarily. It's just that I would've expected to find some blood in his car. And a lot less blood in hers."

"Do you think someone messed with the scene?" I asked.

"Maybe. Sheeley said it probably happened at least a half hour before he spotted it, so somebody could have."

"Or Sheeley could have."

"Well, it seems we know that now, but nobody thought of that back then. Today we expect lawsuits in a case like this, and there'd be all kinds of forensics experts all over the scene and autopsies and measurements and expert evaluations of the evidence to try to determine exactly what happened. We'd know, for instance, if someone had moved the bodies. But thirty years ago we just counted it as a terrible tragedy and tried real hard not to make anything worse for the families that had lost loved ones. It was a different time. And, I must confess, I was as green as could be and only too glad to follow Jack Sheeley's advice so I could get the hell out of there.''

Something occurred to me. ''Did you say no autopsy?''

''Probably not. They weren't as automatic then as they are now. The cause of death was obvious as hell and since there wasn't evidence of alcohol being involved, someone could decide to save the county the expense. Again, the fact that both of them were dead made a lot of things moot.''

''So no one would've known that she'd recently had a baby,'' I said.

Sophie's eyebrows shot up at that, but I figured it was largely for effect. I assumed that she'd already figured out that Paula was the birth mother in the ''adoption thing'' we had talked about at our first meeting.

Frank just shook his head.

After I thanked Frank and he left, Sophie and I read through the accident report together, but we didn't find anything that added to our information, except to realize that the report was more interesting in what it didn't say than in what it did.

If the DA's office was going to abandon their investigation into Jack Sheeley any minute now, as Charlie had suggested, I was going to need Sophie's help to go on, so it was time to tell her the whole story. With my nurse's blessing and with my guardian in attendance at a respectful distance, we went to the hospital cafeteria to have lunch while I brought her up to date. I realized I had been in the hospital too long when I started to see familiar faces among the staff and even the visitors.

We found a remote corner where our conversation wouldn't be overheard above the cafeteria chatter and began to consume our tuna salad sandwiches on institutional whole wheat.

"So what you're looking for is some connection between Jack Sheeley and the baby's father, except we don't know who the baby's father is."

"Was. Sheeley said he's dead."

"So who do you think we're looking for, if not the baby's father?" she asked.

"I think there're two possibilities here. The first is that Sheeley was looking for the 'kid' as he said—it's hard for me to think of Tally as a 'kid,' since she's thirty years old—so he can restore her to the bosom of her family, but I can't square that with what we know about Jack Sheeley. When he said 'It's bye-bye girlie for both of you,' he wasn't talking about a trip to Disneyland."

"It doesn't seem likely. What do you think the other possibility is?"

"I think he was looking for her to keep her from being restored to the bosom of her family. And that plan wouldn't die with him. I think somebody out there cares very much that she not arrive on the family doorstep one day."

"Even after thirty years?"

"Yes, even after thirty years."

Sophie pondered for a while.

"The likeliest place to start is that Cayman Islands thing, to find out who was paying him. If the DA is about to abandon the affair, which seems likely, they may give me access to what they learned from the search warrant. I have an associate who specializes in off-shore shenanigans who might have the Cayman Islands connections we need. Do you want me to proceed on that?"

"I certainly do, unless you decide there's something more promising to pursue."

After lunch, Sophie and I parted company, she to go off and slay the dragons, and me to go back with my guardian to my room. He actually checked out the room before he let me back in, which I found somehow entertaining. Despite what I had been through less than forty-eight hours before, it was still hard to think of myself as a target for desperadoes. Besides, they would hardly benefit from attacking me, because everything I knew a lot of other people knew by now, too. I thought I was pretty safe.

I passed my afternoon tests with flying colors and, after a stern lecture from Doctor Evans on the risks associated with severe head trauma and the possibility of grand mal epilepsy and what symptoms to watch for and what circumstances should make me come running back to him, I got my release.

At six o'clock, Charlie arrived to take me home.

In true hospital fashion, after making me march up and down the hall to demonstrate my fitness to leave, when it came time to leave, they insisted that I sit down and be wheeled out of the hospital. Just before we left the premises, I got parked in a hall with my guardian while Charlie and my nurse went to pick up the doctor's parting instructions. Once again, I found myself wondering at the familiar faces among the people coming and going in the hall. Among others, my cheerful ER guy waved and said he was happy to see me going home so soon.

I signed some forms on a clipboard, Charlie brought the car around, and the nurse and policeman abandoned me to his care. Molly was in the car, and ecstatic to see me. Molly is a fairly reserved dog, so you had to know that all that waggling of the rear end (not just the tail, but the entire back half) meant ecstasy, and I got her trademark tiny little kisses all over my hands and arms. All the way to Charlie's house, I got nudged any time I showed signs of inattention in the head scratching department.

CHARLIE'S HOUSE was in Harrison, not too far from where the diet doctor had once lived and loved. It was fairly imposing—red brick with black-and-white trim in a faintly Georgian style, with two-story white pillars in the front.

"Impressive." I said.

"Not too impressive," he answered. "It's practically the neighborhood slum. After all, we only had one robber baron in the family. My grandfather built it for his young family in nineteen-oh-five, and my father managed to hold on to it through the depression, although it was touch and go for a while. I don't think either of my children wants it when I go, but maybe they'll have changed their minds by then."

"Let's hope so," I said, thinking of my tiny three-bedroom ranch outside of Boulder, and how you could probably hide the whole thing in Charlie's living room.

Once inside, Molly acted like she owned the place, which, to all intents and purposes, she did. Martha had already discovered that Molly loved to be picked up and carried so she could look out on the world over your shoulder and it was evident to me that I was going to have to intervene soon if Molly was ever to get any exercise again.

The furnishings in Charlie's house were contemporary, comfortable, and informal, and I was more than happy not to be back in the Hutch Heights with that special furniture they design for upscale hotel rooms that looks comfortable and inviting but isn't.

Over dinner, Charlie and I brought each other up to date on the day's happenings. The search warrant had turned up lots of papers, including tax returns that showed that Sheeley had reported and paid taxes on all his earnings from the Cayman Islands, but nothing that revealed much. Charlie thought that the investigation would probably be cut off by the next day, if it hadn't been already.

I then told him about Frank Geoghegan and turning Sophie loose on the Cayman Islands connection.

Thoroughly exhausted by nine o'clock, I crawled into bed and Molly took up her usual position on a pillow of her own next to mine. I didn't ask her where she had spent the last two nights because, if there had been any disloyalty, I didn't want to know.

TWENTY-ONE

MOLLY ALREADY KNEW the routine of the household and had evidently found someone else to handle her first outing of the day. At eight o'clock, she came bouncing back in with Martha, who carried a breakfast tray and a message that the doctor had ordered exercise and the judge was ready whenever I was for our first walk of the day. I groaned.

Martha grinned. "You might as well do it; he's not going to go away."

I was grateful when Martha insisted on staying with me to assist me in those things that were awkward and painful for me to accomplish on my own. As she was drying my hair, she said to my image in the mirror, "The judge's really quite smitten, you know. I haven't seen him like this in years. Not since his wife died."

"He's smitten with this?" I said, pointing to my battered face and technicolor eyes.

"I don't think that has a whole lot to do with it," she said in return.

We decided between us that no amount of makeup was going to hide the carnage and could possibly make it look worse, so we settled on just a pair of sunglasses, because Martha insisted there wasn't a single veil in the entire house.

It was a glorious morning; the sun was brilliant and the sky bright blue with high, puffy white clouds. The air was soft and sweetly scented with some late summer flower and there was the gentlest of breezes. We went out the back of the house, cutting through a neighbor's yard—which Charlie assured me was a tradition of long standing. We stopped to chat with that self-same neighbor, who was tending to an enormous bed of rhododendrons. I could only imagine how spectacular they would look in the spring.

Our progress around the block was fairly slow, given the number of neighbors we had to stop and chat with (all of whom seemed fully conversant with my recent history; evidently even Harrison has its back-fence gossips) and the minutiae that Molly had to investigate. Thus, it was almost an hour later when we turned the corner onto Charlie's block.

A fashionably-green sedan was parked across from Charlie's drive. As we approached, it started up, hung a U-turn, and sped past us.

"Why, that's—" I started to say, and then stopped, because I realized that I didn't know who it was.

"Who was he?" Charlie asked.

"I don't know; I just thought he looked familiar. If I stop thinking about it now, maybe it will come to me later."

Charlie's study was the perfect place to spend the rest of the morning. It was done in warm woods and caramel-colored leather, with an important-looking blue, taupe, and cream oriental rug on the floor. While Charlie worked at his desk, I lounged on the leather couch, my laptop opened on a table designed specifically for couch laptoppers. I suppose some people actually put them on their laps, but then most people have more lap than I do. Molly took turns snuggling up against me for attention and dashing through the open French doors to the terrace to warn off any feline would-be intruders.

The phone call that ended that pleasant idyll came for Charlie shortly after lunch. I wasn't paying any attention to his conversation, so I was a little surprised when he raised his voice a notch and said, "Yes, I'll be there in an hour and a half. Thank you very much."

He had my full attention as he hung up and turned to me. "That was St. Vincent's. Sheila's been the victim of a hit-and-run in the Village. She's still unconscious but they expect her to come out of it soon. She has a broken leg but that seems to be the worst of it. They found my name and number on a piece of paper in her pocket. I told them I'd be right down."

"Well, I'm coming, too," I said, getting up from the couch.

"Do you feel up to it?"

"Good grief, you didn't ask me if I was up to a forced march around Harrison this morning. Of course I'm up to it."

ON THE WAY to the city, we pointed out to each other various landmarks from earlier years and piled anecdote on anecdote as people do who are eager to get to know each other. At the hospital, Charlie dropped me off while he went to park the car. After stopping at a few desks and getting directions in this ancient and massive pile of a hospital, I found myself in the orthopedics department, where the nursing staff, once satisfied that I was who I claimed to be, let me into the cubicle where a doctor was putting the finishing touches on a cast on Sheila's leg. She gave me a wan smile as I came around the edge of the curtain.

"I need a poor baby," she said.

"Poor baby," I responded, putting as much feeling into it as I could. I took her hand and held it.

"Now I feel better. They give you excellent care here, but they don't know about the poor baby part."

"What happened?" I asked.

"I don't really know. I stepped off the curb at the corner of Bleecker and Sullivan and this car came out of nowhere. The man behind me grabbed me and probably saved my life. He and a cab driver brought me over here. They're probably still outside somewhere, because they said they wouldn't leave until someone came to look after me."

"I'll go find them as soon as Charlie gets here," I said.

"The judge is coming?"

"Yes; he's parking the car."

"They told me they called him before I woke up— I had his phone number in my pocket. I called Mom as soon as I could, and Teddy's coming down to get me, but it'll take him three or four hours." Most of Sheila's family, including my ex-sister-in-law, Sheila's mother, lived within a few miles of each other in an area near Scranton, Pennsylvania. Teddy was her cousin. I remembered him as large, friendly, and very protective of his favorite cousin.

"You're going home?"

"Well, I can't negotiate a third-floor walkup very well in this getup," she said, gesturing at the foot-to-mid-thigh cast on her left leg.

"If you don't feel up to that long drive back, we can find someplace else for you to stay tonight."

"No, it's not that bad. Just a crack, really. They'll give me some knockout pills before I go and I can just crash on the back seat. Tomorrow will probably be worse than today and I'll be much better off there than here.''

Charlie stuck his head around the curtain and said, "Hi, Sheila. We've got to stop meeting like this," and she laughed. Then he said to me, "Lexy, there are some people out here you need to talk to."

Out in the aisle, there was a small knot of people close by Sheila's cubicle, one of them a uniformed policeman. Charlie and I joined them.

"Are you the people who rescued my niece?" I asked of the other two.

"Yes, I'm Neil MacAndrews and this is Dominick Fiore," said one of them, with what I took to be a faint Scots accent. Neil was slender and tweedily elegant and Dominick was plump and cordially rumpled—as unlikely a pair as you could meet, but they seemed to have forged a bond.

"Lexy Connor," I answered as I shook their hands and that of the officer, who introduced himself as Peter Fonseca. "I can't tell you how grateful I am."

"We're just glad to hear she's going to be all right," Neil said, "except for the leg, of course. I was afraid things might be much worse."

"Does anyone know what happened?"

Dominick spoke up, "It was intentional."

"Intentional?" I said, and the shock I felt must have been apparent in my voice, because Dominick nodded vigorously.

"This car had been double-parked and it suddenly pulled out just in front of my cab—like it was waiting for her. When the young lady stepped off the curb, he gunned the motor and headed right at her. If Neil here hadn't pulled her back, the car could have killed her. He just kept on going. I was going to chase him, but he ran the light and the cross traffic was already moving when I got to the intersection. So I decided the best thing for me to do was to get her to a hospital as fast as possible. Neil and I put her in the cab and brought her here.''

"I'm afraid I drew the same conclusion—it was deliberate," Neil said. "When I pulled her back, we fell over backward and sort of twisted and banged into a parked car. The car didn't touch her or at least I don't think it did, so I'm afraid I'm responsible for her broken leg and her being unconscious.''

"Hardly. You saved her life. But who would have—" and I stopped, because I couldn't even think "tried to kill Sheila.''

The policeman said, "We were thinking you could help us on that one.''

I shrugged and shook my head in disbelief. I didn't know all the details of Sheila's life, but I thought I'd know if anyone hated her enough to try to kill her.

"We have officers canvassing the block to see if any witnesses made the license plate, but all we have at the moment is that it was a large, late model, dark green car.''

My knees suddenly turned to jelly and I grabbed Charlie's arm. "I need to sit down," I said. Charlie assisted me to a bench by the nurse's station.

"The green car," I finally said after Dominick brought me a cup of water. "They think Sheila is Tally. They're not after me now. They're after her. Tally, I mean. She was always the real objective anyway.''

Charlie nodded at me and took the police officer aside while Neil and Dominick hovered over me. "I'm quite all right really," I told them. "We just think this attack on Sheila may be tied to an attack on me a few days ago. The idea came as something of a shock to me.''

Charlie came back and told Neil and Dominick, ''Sheila's cousin is coming from Scranton to take her home where she'll be safe and well looked after; he'll be here in a few hours. Lexy and I will stay with her until he comes. For the time being, the hospital is going to tell anyone who calls or visits that she is in intensive care in critical condition. That should keep anyone from trying to find her elsewhere, and we'd appreciate it if you would stick to that story until we tell you otherwise.''

They nodded solemnly.

''I know the police have them, but could we have your addresses and phone numbers? I know that Sheila's family will want to thank you,'' I said. Neil took out a case and presented me with a crisp business card. Dominick pulled a grubby ''Reddi Radio Taxi Service'' card from his pocket and wrote his information on the back. They stopped to say goodbye to Sheila and then went on their way.

''Boy, she was lucky to get them,'' I said and Charlie agreed. We went back into Sheila's cubicle to keep her company until Teddy came. I told her my theory of why she had been attacked and Charlie told her what was being done to protect her.

''Wow,'' was all she could say when we were finished.

''What do you need to get from your apartment?'' I said. ''It's not safe for you to go back there today. Whoever he is, he probably followed you there when Mike took you home from the hospital in White Plains, so he knows where you live.''

''I've already called one of my friends. She's going

to get what I need and take it to her place and Teddy
and I will pick it up there on our way home. I don't
need much, because I have clothes and everything at
Mom's place, and most of my clothes I can't wear
anyway. I'll be just fine as soon as I'm home."

When Teddy arrived several hours later, they had
him pull his car into the ambulance bay. We said goodbye to Sheila in her room and left—hospital security
personnel would take her by a route through the innards
of the hospital so that no observer would realize she
was leaving or be able to track where she was going.
When I commented on how efficiently they handled
this, a nurse said, "When you deal with a lot of battered wives, you develop ways of keeping people out
of sight. This is actually routine for us."

ON THE TRIP BACK to Harrison, I felt my fury mounting.
The attack on Sheila outraged me far more than the
attack on me. I had, at least, gone looking for trouble.
And my attacker had certainly gotten his comeuppance.
But Sheila was just a case of badly mistaken identity.
Charlie and I kept tossing back and forth what the attack could mean for my investigation. As if we knew.
All we knew for certain was that having Sheeley in his
grave wasn't going to be enough to protect Tally, or
whoever they thought might be Tally. And we knew
that they had connected me with the woman they were
looking for. Enough digging in my background could
yield the real Tally, not to mention that they might
bump off every young woman I've ever known in the
process.

I had a greater sense of urgency than ever, and no
plan whatsoever to do anything about it. Charlie wisely
counseled that I probably ought to sleep on it and, after

a long conversation with Tally in which she urged me to quit before anyone else was hurt and I explained to her that I couldn't quit with things left in a worse state than I had found them, that's what I did.

a long conversation naturally to which she urged me
to get before anyone else was away and I explained to
her that I could... ...that ...was sure
that ...

TWENTY-TWO

THINGS WERE fairly quiet the next day. Sheila was safely with her family in Pennsylvania. The hospital was advising callers that she was in critical condition and could not be visited. A visitor, a woman, had come looking for the person who was hit in the Village the day before, but left again before anyone could notify security. No one had a good description of her except that she was well-dressed. The police so far had not found any witnesses to the accident who got the license plate numbers or who felt they could identify the driver. The press had been turned off completely, or maybe they had never picked up the story in the first place, which was fine with me. I guess, in New York City, an almost-hit and run resulting in a broken leg wasn't going to grab the front page.

Once again, we were in Charlie's study. He was reading some fat legal book and I was laptopping on his neat little table again.

I caught up on several days' worth of e-mail. Then I played back the recording of Sheeley's visit to my hotel room, so I could hear what he'd said while I was unconscious, but I didn't learn anything new from it. Even the expletives, of which there were many, were old hat.

That done, I started flipping idly through the clippings that Celie had printed out for me on Saturday, a lifetime ago, this time stopping to read the ones I hadn't read before.

And there it was, and had been all along. In the article about the merging of Burns, Prescott & Prescott at the retirement of the last partner—the one Celie had requested on her own, without my prompting.

"Charlie," I cried out.

"What is it?"

"They knew each other."

"Who knew each other?"

"Paula and Prescott."

He came to my side and I showed him the clipping.

"Look, here in the article about the law firm being merged, it says that the spokesman for Prescott was from the New York office of the public relations firm, Bartlett and Ruskie. Bartlett and Ruskie is where Paula worked, except she worked in White Plains. But they knew each other. Of course they did. They could easily have met. Paula could have gone on an errand to New York or something like that, or he could have come to the White Plains office. That's what Sheeley meant when he got sarcastic about my saying that I didn't know who the father was. And he said the father was dead, too. He saw all this stuff on Prescott that Celie had printed and assumed I knew its significance. That's why he decided he needed to kill me—because he thought I knew Prescott was the father."

"You may be right. And if you are, that explains where a fortune big enough to be worth chasing after for thirty years may lie."

"A lot of money?"

"Carloads."

"But he killed her," I said, thinking about what a blow that would be to Tally.

"We don't know that," he said. "We don't really know what happened out there that night, and if Sheeley had time to doctor the scene, no one will ever know.''

"I just can't believe that I didn't realize a lot sooner that he was the one. Sheeley practically spelled it out for me.''

"Don't blame yourself; you only learned Prescott existed a few days ago, and a lot has happened in between.''

"But I do blame myself. If it weren't for Celie Johnson, I wouldn't have figured it out today, either.''

"What do you plan to do now?''

"Okay, let's assume for the sake of argument that it is the Prescott fortune that's at stake here, and Prescott's father who would leave it to Tally.''

"That's a possibility.''

"Then the quickest way to make Tally safe is to make her grandfather aware of her existence, don't you think?''

"But what if he's the source of the problem? What if Sheeley came from him?''

"I'll have to take that chance. I don't know any other way to move forward. I can't just wait for them to find Tally to see who they are. So I need to go see old Prescott.''

"Foster, he goes by 'Foster.'''

"Okay, I need to go see Foster.''

"I can arrange that, but only if we go together.''

"I was sort of hoping you'd say that.''

Charlie went back to his desk and hauled out the biggest Rolodex I had ever seen.

"Holy Toledo,'' I said.

"My secretary at the courthouse never let a single fact escape her. She retired when I did, so I got the benefit of her zealotry; anybody who has ever walked into a courtroom in New York State is probably in here. Ah, yes, here he is. Larchmont." He dialed a number and I listened to his half of the conversation.

"I'd like to talk to Foster Prescott, please… No, it's a confidential matter… Yes, thank you… Foster! This is Charlie Seabrook. Do you remember me?… Fine, just fine… No, I retired from the bench last year… I'm keeping busy with a little bit here and a little bit there… Some writing. Some teaching. Nothing too strenuous… I'd like to come and see you, if I may, about an old legal matter… I'd rather wait and tell you in person… No, alone. It is extremely confidential… Yes, I'd prefer that… Fine, I'm looking forward to seeing you, too. It's been much too long… Until then… Goodbye."

"It's on?" I asked.

"It's on for three this afternoon. And he'll be there alone except for the servants." He picked up the phone again, saying, "Just as a precaution, I'm going to ask Sophie and one of her associates to be on standby."

"Do you think that's necessary?" I said.

"No, just wise."

TWENTY-THREE

AFTER LUNCH, which I was too excited to do more than just pick at, I went to get dressed for our afternoon's outing. I wasn't quite sure what one wore to a surprise! - your - granddaughter - is - alive - and - well - and - living - in - Palo - Alto party, but finally decided that my new black silk shantung struck just the right note of formal solemnity with elegance. In any event, it was the best I was going to do with the bulk of my wardrobe sitting two thousand miles away.

There was nothing that could be done about the comic-opera coloring of my face, so I just decided a really well-bred person would ignore it and popped my sunglasses on.

There was little conversation as we took the Hutch south to Weaver Street and then took Weaver Street into Larchmont.

When we found the address, we also found Sophie sitting in a car by the driveway. With her was no less than Frank Geoghegan. We pulled up alongside them and spoke briefly.

"I thought Frank might like to be in on this one," she said.

"Well, I'm sorry to say that I hope Frank has an uneventful afternoon," Charlie answered with a grin.

This was no mere house; it was an estate, and the house was a mansion in a toned-down Italian palazzo style. It was set well back from the road, and was surrounded by a tall wrought-iron fence, surmounted with very unfriendly looking spikes. The gate was opened electrically after Charlie addressed the intercom and said, "Judge Seabrook to see Mr. Prescott" in a voice that indicated years of experience in sounding commanding when circumstances called for it.

As we pulled up to the front of the house with Sophie's car behind us, the front door was opened by a slender young black woman in a black dress and white apron, which I realized with a shock was a uniform. Uniformed servants were beyond my experience, but then so was a private home like this. I have been in houses as splendid on any number of occasions, but they had all been taken over by institutions because families could no longer afford the upkeep, let alone the taxes.

We left Sophie and Frank sitting in the driveway; she handed Charlie something small that he slipped in his pocket.

"What's that?" I said.

"A panic button. You know what those are for."

"I sure do."

We were met in the enormous marbled front hall by an elderly man in a wheelchair. He looked fragile, but his voice was hearty when he greeted us.

"Charlie, it's really good to see you. And who is this?" he said, turning to me.

"This is Lexy Connor; she's an associate of mine. I think she'd want you to know that she's recuperating from a nasty incident and doesn't normally look like somebody's punching bag." I was glad that was out of the way. There was going to be enough to deal with in the next hour or so without his wondering how I came to be rainbow-colored.

"I'm pleased to meet you, Mr. Prescott," I said.

"Foster, please. And may I call you Lexy?"

"By all means."

His handshake was also strong, which encouraged me; I felt he was going to need all his strength this afternoon.

"Let's go to my study," he said, preceding us down the hall and into a beautiful, book-lined study. His was done in darker woods and leather than Charlie's, and the furnishings were simply drop-dead gorgeous. The desk alone was a masterpiece of the cabinetmaker's art. Tall windows looked out on the sailors on Long Island Sound, where a day that had started beautiful was now even more so. It was hard to imagine that it was only two weeks ago since I'd sat looking at much the same scene and choosing high schools to visit.

Foster wheeled himself behind the desk and motioned us to the chairs across from him.

"Now what's this all about, Charlie?"

"This is Lexy's story," Charlie said, and turned and nodded to me.

"It's about your granddaughter," I said.

He looked at me sharply. "How do you know I have a granddaughter?" he asked. At least he didn't deny having a granddaughter, which I had been afraid he might.

"'Know' is probably too strong a term. I believe, based on circumstantial evidence and some conjecture, that your son had a daughter, born shortly before he died."

His voice shook a little when he said, "What about my granddaughter?"

"We know who she is and where she is," I said.

He looked at Charlie and said, "Is this true?"

Charlie nodded, "It's true."

"Have you the proof?"

This time Charlie looked at me with a quizzical expression, as if to say "What's he talking about?" I wasn't sure I knew, either, but I took a stab at it.

"Not with us," I answered. "It's in another state, but I can have it here in two days, and I can describe it to you now. It's an inexpensive woman's ring with a blue stone and 'PJ' engraved on the inside."

He looked at me for a long minute and then sat back in his chair and stared at the ceiling as he wiped his hand over his forehead.

"Then it is my granddaughter. I've never told anyone what the proof would be, or even that there was proof. That was the only way I could be sure that it hadn't been manufactured. But that's how the ring has been described and you couldn't know that if you hadn't seen it. I'm satisfied."

So the ring wasn't a clue at all; instead, it was the proof of Tally's parentage.

He sat forward again and went on, "But we've been looking for her for thirty years. How did you find her? Where is she? When can I see her?"

"I didn't find her; I've known her for twenty years. My problem has been finding you. But she's also in another part of the country, and I can't let you know where she is or have her come here until I'm certain that it's safe," I answered.

"Safe? What do you mean by that?"

"You may have been looking for her for thirty years with the best of intentions, but someone else has been looking for her for the same thirty years to make certain that you'd never find her."

This took a long time to sink in. The signs of conflict in his face were painful to watch. He finally spoke.

"What do I have to do to assure you that she will be safe?"

"We have to identify the people who are likely to do her harm and"—I groped for a word—"neutralize them."

"And how do you propose to do that?"

"There are still a lot of holes in this story, but between the two of us, we may have the answers. If you could tell me what you know, it would tell me where I have to start to tell you what I know."

He didn't appear to be particularly thrilled by my idea, but I guess he decided he had nothing to lose by going along with me, because he leaned forward in his chair, placed his elbows on the desk, tented his fingers before him, and began in a monotone, as if reciting it.

"Very well, then. Thirty years ago last June, the police arrived on my doorstep at six in the morning to tell me that my son had been killed in an auto accident on the Taconic Parkway about three hours earlier. I didn't believe them, because I thought my son was upstairs asleep. But they were right.

"I called my daughter-in-law downstairs and she told me that Pres had gone out the evening before and not come back. She hadn't even realized he wasn't back until just then. She was upset, as I was. He was my only child and I had just lost his mother to cancer the year before.

"It was such a shock to my system that I wasn't even able to return to work for over a month. It wasn't until mid-July that I found a letter addressed to me from my son waiting in my office mail. It was postmarked the day he died and was marked to be opened only by me. Rather than sending it out to the house to me, some stupid temp secretary had shoved it in a file folder and forgotten about it.

"I couldn't believe it at first, except that it was unmistakably in Pres's handwriting. I can recite it from memory.

Dear Papa,

I am sorry to go like this without talking to you first, but it seems to be necessary. In a few weeks we should have everything under control and I hope you won't be too unhappy with the way things work out. In the meantime, you ought to know that I have a beautiful baby daughter, only a week old, and I am desperately in love with her beautiful mother.

However, her mother and I will have to be separated from our little darling for a short while, and I wanted you to know about her in case anything happens to our flight. A trusted friend is taking care of her and, if necessary, she will bring her to you. The proof that she is my daughter will be a ring with a blue stone in it and the initials 'PJ' engraved inside.

Please don't say anything to Clarissa yet. I will call her in few days.

Your loving son, Pres.

"That was all it said. I never showed the actual letter to my daughter-in-law because I didn't want her to know he was planning on leaving her. It would only hurt her, and it was bad enough that I had to tell her he had a child out of wedlock. But I've been looking for Pres's daughter ever since. I've spent millions on the search."

"Do you know who the mother was?" I asked.

"No, we never found that out and I never heard from the mother or the friend or anyone else after he was killed."

"Then you don't know that the woman who was killed in the accident was the mother."

I could tell from the shocked look on his face that this thought had never occurred to him.

"But they were in two different cars," he sputtered.

Charlie spoke then, saying, "Foster, are you going to be all right? Can you handle this? There's a lot more to come."

This seemed to have a calming effect—perhaps he was afraid that if he didn't appear able to handle it, we would leave without telling him what he wanted to know.

"I'll be okay, thanks, Charlie. I'll be as strong as I have to be. Please go on, Lexy."

"Well, there's certainly more bad news, but you ought to know up front that your granddaughter is a smart, beautiful, healthy young woman, and a person of great character to boot. She's been my friend since she was a child."

"Thank you for that. What else do you want to know?"

"I want to know what you planned to do if you ever found her, and who would benefit if she was never found, or was found to have died."

"She's my principal heir—she gets the bulk of the estate, after making provision for my daughter-in-law and a few charitable trusts. That's the way my will is written today."

"And if she was never found?"

"If she wasn't located within five years of my death,

the estate would revert to a charitable foundation run by my daughter-in-law.''

''And if she was found to have died?''

His voice dropped to a whisper. ''You mean before I died?''

''Yes.''

''I'd have rewritten my will to leave a larger portion directly to my daughter-in-law and the rest to the charitable foundation she runs.''

''One last question—who have you had searching for your granddaughter?''

''Clarissa's brother.''

''Clarissa?''

''My daughter-in-law, Pres's wife. Her brother is Hatch.''

''Hatch?''

''Hatch Fillmore. He's been heading up the search all these years. They both live here with me so he could devote himself to the search, but he never found her.''

''I think that's probably a good thing,'' I said. ''I don't think that if he had found her, you'd have gotten to see her alive.''

The appalling truth sort of lay there on the desk between us. Then he said, ''Tell me what you know.''

''The mother's name was Paula Chandler. She was a secretary at Bartlett and Ruskie in White Plains, and I think that's how she met your son.'' He nodded at that.

''I don't know how they came to be in two different cars and had that terrible accident on the Taconic, but we do know that the highway patrol officer first on the scene was always involved after that, right up until this weekend, when he shot and killed a young man, did this to me''—I pointed to my face—''and then got

himself shot and killed in a gunfight with the police."
Now he looked hard at my face and I swapped my
sunglasses for my regular glasses so he could better see
what I looked like.

"Your granddaughter was in the care of a trusted
friend. After the accident, for some reason that friend
decided the baby was in danger and she took great
pains to hide her, including going into hiding herself
for the past thirty years. I assume she believed that
there was great risk in bringing the child to you. I
didn't know her, but everything I've heard about her
suggests that she was a woman of great kindness and
integrity. She certainly didn't act out of any selfish interest. She gave the baby to a wonderful couple who
raised her as their own."

"You speak of her as if she were dead," he said.

"She is, at the hands of the same person who did
this to me."

"And who is that?"

"Jack Sheeley."

"Sheeley? Good God, I've been such an idiot!"

I pretty much agreed with him, but I politely asked,
"Why do you say that?"

"He was Hatch's chief investigator, supposedly
searching diligently for my granddaughter. He was always dashing around the country investigating 'leads.'
Year after year, he's sat where you're sitting now and
told me how some new lead had turned out to be false
after all, and he was playing me for a fool the whole
time. Do you think Hatch was in on it? Sorry, that was
a damn stupid question. Of course Hatch was in on it,
and Clarissa has to have been, too. She kept telling me
she wanted to find the girl because his daughter was

all she had left of Pres, and I was fool enough to believe her.''

Then, piece by piece, I rebuilt the case for him, starting with Tally showing up with the note from Dolly and finding the ring in the jewelry box, and finishing with that morning's discovery that there was a connection between Bartlett & Ruskie and Burns, Prescott & Prescott.

I concluded by saying, ''It seems to me to be an unavoidable conclusion that the danger to Tally comes from this house.'' He sat there nodding his head for a long time. I couldn't even guess what images of the last thirty years were passing before him.

The light was dim in the study by now because the windows came into the house's shadow. Charlie got up and turned on some lamps, and we all sat looking at each other for a long uncomfortable moment.

''Where are they?'' Charlie asked.

''Out somewhere together. They spend most of their time together. They should be home any time now; we generally dine at seven.''

''Do you mind if I bring in my backups?''

''Not at all. I think we'd better have them.''

Charlie went to get Sophie and Frank, I went to find a powder room, and Foster went to ask for some refreshments to be brought in.

TWENTY-FOUR

WHEN WE WERE all back in the study together, we
made desultory conversation, but it didn't mask the fact
that all we were doing was waiting and listening. Sophie did manage to ask Foster if he knew anything
about the Cayman Islands connection. He said he
didn't, but he suspected it was a way of hiding from
him the amounts that were going to Sheeley. He
thought he was paying a whole crew of investigators,
with Sheeley as their leader, but that now seemed unlikely. It didn't take a whole crew of investigators to
not find anything, he added ruefully.

The maid knocked and stuck her head in the door,
"They're back, sir," she said.

"Thanks, Sandy. Tell Clarissa I'd like to see her,
please." She nodded and withdrew.

A few minutes later, the door opened again and, as
if on cue, both Charlie and Frank rose from their chairs.

From across the room, Clarissa Fillmore Prescott
looked very handsome, perhaps even beautiful, but
when she got closer, you could see the ravages of too
many trips under the plastic surgeon's knife—a face
with skin so taut that it looked as if a smile, or any
genuine expression of feeling, would be painful. She
was wearing my usual uniform—camel slacks, cream
silk blouse, and a navy silk blazer. No imagination
whatsoever.

"Papa, you didn't tell me there'd be company." She
surveyed us briefly and then settled her gaze on Char-

lie. She did a double-take, but recovered quickly and advanced on him, saying, "Charlie Seabrook, you old bastard! What brings you to us?" as she took his hand in both of hers and kissed the air around him.

Charlie said, "Hello, Clarissa. Let me introduce some associates of mine, Lexy Connor, Sophie Hirsch, and Frank Geoghegan."

Black silk shantung notwithstanding, she looked at me as if I was something the cat had dragged in and pointedly ignored my extended hand. I was fairly certain she thought she'd catch fat if she touched me. That was okay, because I didn't really want to touch her, either. She nodded curtly at Sophie and Frank. I thought, but wasn't sure, that my name might have meant something to her, but it was clear that she didn't consider Sophie and Frank to be much more than furniture. She turned back toward Charlie and Foster and said, "To what do we owe the pleasure?"

Foster spoke first. "They've found Pres's daughter."

"Oh, my goodness! I must sit down!" she exclaimed and sat down in the chair Charlie had risen from at her entrance. "Is she here? I can't wait to meet her. Oh, Foster, this is such wonderful news!"

Since we all knew this to be an act, we were enthralled by the performance—all except Foster, who scowled. "Cut it out, Clarissa. I know the truth. I know all about you and Hatch and Sheeley." He then turned to Frank and said, "Would you mind stepping out into the hall and asking Sandy to invite Hatch to join us? You just might go along with her, too, in case he thinks he wants to say no."

Frank left the room.

Clarissa was trying to decide between wounded innocence and stony silence, and apparently the latter won out because after one "This is ridiculous," she didn't say anything more. We all sat in silence waiting for Frank to return with Hatch.

When they did come in a few minutes later, it was my turn to do a double-take.

"Charlie," I said, "he's the one. He was at the hospital—at the nurse's station on my floor, in the cafeteria when Sophie and I were having lunch, by the door when we left, and he was the one outside your house yesterday morning in the green car. And that means he's the one who tried to kill Sheila."

Hatch evidently decided on straight denial, because he immediately said, "I don't know what you're talking about. What hospital? Who's Sheila?"

"Sheila is my niece, and she's not Pres's missing daughter. But you thought she was and so you tried to run her down in Greenwich Village yesterday."

"It wasn't me," he sputtered.

"That's not important right now," Charlie answered. "If necessary, we can find other witnesses who can place you at the hospital. And the hit-and-run—those witnesses can probably identify you, too."

"It wasn't a hit-and-run; I didn't hit anything."

"But not for want of trying," I said.

Hatch turned to Clarissa and said, "Rissa, who are these people?"

Clarissa just shrugged.

"They're the people who have found Pres's daughter," Foster spoke now.

"You mean she's been found? That's great! Where is she?" he said, recovering himself enough to speak with the same feigned enthusiasm his sister had shown us earlier.

"I don't know. They won't tell me until the threat to her safety is removed."

Hatch ignored the last remark and said, "How do you know it's her? God knows, we've had enough false leads over the years."

"I know it's her. There is a way of proving it; there has always been a way of proving it, and thank God I was smart enough not to tell you two about it. And I know why we've had so many false leads over the years. It's because you and your so-called investigator have been generating them for your entertainment and the lightening of my pockets."

"Now wait a minute," Hatch began, and started moving toward Foster's desk. Frank unceremoniously stepped in front of him and pushed him into a chair. He leaned into Hatch's face and said, "What's your connection with Jack Sheeley?" Frank wasn't going to get over being Sheeley's dupe any time soon.

"I hired his detective agency," Hatch answered.

"No, I mean, where did you meet him? Before that."

"His kid brother and I played high school football together in the Bronx. Jack was a city cop back then and used to buy our beer for us because we were too young to buy it ourselves. I always went on the beer runs with him because I was the one with the money."

"How did Sheeley know you were connected with Prescott?"

Here Hatch went pale and started to sputter a little. "I don't know that he did. I just hired him, that's all."

My mind flashed on something that Sheeley had said in my hotel room: "The father is just as dead as the mother. They saw to that."

Suddenly a new scenario for the accident began to

emerge. I turned to Frank and said, somewhat incoherently, "Frank, the accident—that night. Could they have both been in the Alfa? Could someone have moved the bodies to make it look like Prescott was driving the Mercedes?"

Frank nodded at me. "It could have been that way. That would explain a lot."

I looked again at Hatch, who obviously knew what night and what accident we were talking about.

"You were there," I cried. "On the Taconic that night. You were driving the Mercedes. They were both in the Alfa."

"Oh, no, you're not going to pin that on me, too. I didn't get there until afterward. I couldn't keep up with the Mercedes. She was driving the Mercedes and she was hell-bent to catch them." He jerked his thumb toward Clarissa and my eyes followed. "It was all over by the time I got there. They were going to go to the Dominican Republic and she wasn't having any of it. We were just lucky that when a cop showed up, it was Sheeley."

I heard Foster gasp, but I couldn't take my eyes off Clarissa to look at him.

"Shut up, you idiot," Clarissa barked, a little too late. "They don't know anything."

Charlie spoke up now, in the authoritative voice that I was coming to recognize as the judge at work, "We know much more than you realize. We know you conspired with Jack Sheeley to defraud Foster Prescott. As conspirators, you are also responsible for the murder of Dolly Miller in Los Angeles and for the murder of Johnny Dorset and the attempt on the life of Lexy Connor here in Westchester, not to mention the attempt on Sheila Connor in New York City yesterday. We have a full audio record of everything Sheeley said before he was killed, and it implicates you two. We have no need to be able to prove that you killed Pres and Paula Chandler, as well. The only way to save yourselves now is for one of you to get the jump on the other in turning state's evidence.'' He turned to Frank and Sophie and said, ''If you would, please, I think we should separate them now and keep them separated until the police arrive. Frank, do you have any connections among the Larchmont police that we could exercise now to get them here in a hurry?''

Frank grinned, ''I sure do,'' and Charlie handed him his cell phone.

''Do it,'' Charlie said.

THE DOMINICAN REPUBLIC was the venue of choice for New Yorkers wanting a fast divorce in those days, closer and far quicker than some of the other divorce mills. There was no waiting period involved. The divorces wouldn't hold up if contested in New York, but perhaps Pres and Paula considered it a starting point. They could have been married there on the same day they got Pres's divorce, so at least she would have her wedding ring to take home to her family, even if it wasn't recognized as valid in the State of New York.

WITHIN AN HOUR, Clarissa and Hatch were in the custody of the Larchmont police and Sophie and Frank had gone to the police station to make the formal complaint. They would most likely be out again before the end of the evening, but Foster said they were under no circumstances to return to the house and he would have their personal belongings ready to send wherever they directed.

Foster and Charlie and I were back in his study, munching sandwiches that Sandy had brought without being asked.

Foster broke the silence, saying, "I should have known. I think in some ways I did know, but I didn't want to admit it to myself. It's like someone not willing to admit to a spouse's infidelity because then they'd have to do something about it. But even if I had figured out that the search for Pres's daughter was a fraud, I would never have dreamed Clarissa actually killed him."

"We don't look for such evil in the people we know and love," I answered. "And most likely she didn't mean to kill them, but only to stop him from leaving her."

"I don't know much about criminal law," Foster said to Charlie, "what will happen to them?"

"I doubt very much that we'll be able to make anything stick about the incident on the Taconic. Too long ago and no evidence. We can believe we know what happened, but convincing a jury beyond a reasonable doubt seems unlikely. If I were the prosecutor I wouldn't try it. No, the best bet is the conspiracy to defraud. They may try to tie in the killings of Dolly Miller and Johnny Dorset and the attempts on Lexy and Sheila, but it might be hard to convince a jury that they knew what Sheeley was about and even though the law says they didn't have to know, juries are tough on that one. I think it's likely that we'll get some prison time, but not a whole lot."

Then Foster turned to me. "Now will you tell me where she is?"

"I'll do better than that," I said. "If you give me a little privacy first, I'll let you talk to her yourself."

"We'll be in the next room when you're ready," Foster replied and promptly left the room with Charlie in tow.

Tally answered the phone on the second ring.

"It's all over," I announced. "The bad guys are in the lock-up and your granddaddy can't wait to meet you."

"Are you okay?" she asked.

"I'm dancing on air. I solved this damn thing, with a lot of help from a lot of terrific people, I might add."

Step by step, I took her through the day, starting with my going through the clippings that morning. Finally, I called Foster in and handed him the phone. "Her name is Tally—short for Thalia—Richard, and she lives in Palo Alto, California." Charlie and I left them alone together.

THE NEXT DAY Charlie and I had nothing to do until the evening, when we would pick up Tally and Hunter at La Guardia. Debbie had been enlisted to pick up the jewelry box and deliver it to FedEx for delivery on Friday. Even though Foster was insisting he didn't have to see the ring, I thought he'd ultimately want it in his hands. Florrie was driving back to Santa Barbara with the girls and the good news for Madelyn that it was safe to return to her own home.

I had called Maria Rivers to tell her that there was no more risk to what was left of her family and told her Dolly's secret. At her request, I promised I would bring Tally to meet her as soon as I could.

I didn't think Lucy Baker would be willing to talk to me on the phone, so I was postponing that call in hopes that Tally would agree to just drop in on her. I figured seeing what Tally looked like would do more for my credibility than anything I could say.

Once more, we were lounging in Charlie's study, ignoring the drizzly weather outside, when I must have dozed off. I awoke to find him leaning over me, supporting his weight on one arm resting on the back of the sofa.

"Hi," I said.

"Hi. How are you feeling?"

"Much better than I look. I actually feel pretty good."

"I'm glad to hear it. Sometimes I wish I weren't such a gentleman."

"Why's that?"

"Because I've been having very ungentlemanly thoughts about you for a week now."

I reached up and put my hand around his neck and pulled his head down to where I could whisper in his ear, "Let yourself go."

TWENTY-FIVE

AFTER TWO DAYS of rainy weather, Saturday proved to be another glorious day.

I kissed Charlie goodbye and drove down to Larchmont to pick up Tally at Foster's house. Hunter had already left that morning to return to Santa Barbara, satisfied that Tally was safe and happy in Foster's hands.

Tally had with her three enormous bouquets of fall flowers—"Foster insisted," she laughed. "I think I have every bloom and bud in the garden here." The car was filled with the spicy odor of carnations and the glory of mums of every description.

THE NEW YORK STATE parkways ban commercial traffic and were laid out in an earlier age when politicians and engineers thought that people traveling by car would want to enjoy the scenic beauty of a place. Their crowning achievement in this regard is the Taconic State Parkway.

The Taconic is born just north of White Plains. It winds its way northward from there, roughly bisecting the narrow strip of New York State between the Hudson River on the west and Connecticut and then Massachusetts on the right. Some eighty miles later, it ends at Interstate 90, which will take you to Albany on the one hand and Boston, much farther away, on the other.

This journey takes it through lushly forested rolling hills, offering occasional spectacular vistas when the road rises high on the side of a steep hill.

Our first destination was a mile marker on the south-bound side of the Taconic, just south of where it crosses the border from Putnam into Westchester County. This was a necessary pilgrimage for both of us, perhaps Tally more than I, but not much more.

There was a railing there now which probably hadn't been there thirty years ago. The parkways had been engineered originally for speeds of forty to forty-five miles per hour, and much had been done over the years to make them safer for the cruising speeds that present-day drivers favored. The addition of guardrails was one of them.

We parked on the shoulder, climbed over the railing, and went down the steep slope. Tally picked the like-liest looking tree, a sturdy old oak, and rested one of her bouquets at its foot.

"I had no idea this place could be so beautiful," she murmured. "I know you and Mom used to carry on about how pretty it was around here, but this is unbe-lievable. If it had to be anywhere, I guess I'm glad it was here."

Just then a voice called out, "Is everything all right down there?"

We turned to see a state highway patrol officer stand-ing next to the guardrail and peering down at us.

"Yes, officer," I called back. "Everything's fine. Some friends were killed at this spot thirty years ago, and we're just, well, visiting."

"Ah. Do you need anything?"

"No, we're fine, thank you."

"Okay, but be careful pulling back onto the road; some people come through here awful fast."

I said I would, and he went on his way.

We climbed back up to the road and perched on the

guardrail for a while, each of us silently entertaining our own ghosts.

Finally she said, "He really loved her. Foster showed me the letter last night."

"I think he did, too. God only knows what being married to Clarissa must have been like."

"Is she really that awful?" Tally asked.

"Well, I've only seen her the one time, but she seemed pretty evil to me. She has to have been the force behind everything because she was the one who stood to benefit, and if we are to believe Hatch, she drove the Mercedes and rammed that poor little Alfa right off the road. Do you have any idea how small an Alfa like that was? They didn't have a prayer."

"I wonder what happened to set everything off that night."

"I've been wondering, too. Are you interested in my speculation?"

"Sure."

"Somehow—maybe they followed him up there—Clarissa and Hatch found Pres and Paula together in Rhinebeck. They were probably getting ready to leave for the Dominican Republic. They were certainly headed somewhere on an airplane, because that was in the note your father sent your grandfather. Clarissa might not even have known about you at that point—maybe Dolly had already taken you to keep until they came back. Anyway, there must have been a showdown of some sort, and Pres and Paula took off in the Alfa with Clarissa in pursuit in the Mercedes. I figure Hatch came along behind in the car that Clarissa and Hatch had taken to Rhinebeck. Clarissa caught up with Pres and Paula here and rammed them off the road. She may even have had her seatbelt fastened, and, according to Frank, she could well have walked away without a scratch. I think Hatch and Clarissa were still at the scene when Jack Sheeley came along. That it was Sheeley could have been just a coincidence, but of course Hatch knew him, and they cooked up something and Hatch and Clarissa went on their way. Sheeley doctored the scene to fit the scenario they wanted and then called for backup.''

"What about Dolly and me?''

"Well, we'll never really know what happened there, because you're the only witness still alive, but Dolly knew Susan from having worked for her family before, and somehow she convinced Susan that you were in danger, which she was certainly right about, and Susan and Peter took you to California with them. Quite likely Dolly went with them, as well. Maybe Dolly went on to live in Gilroy so she could be near you.

"Sheeley said when he went to Rhinebeck you were gone; he probably didn't go to Rhinebeck until after Foster got the letter and Hatch set him on your trail, which would have been a whole month later. Knowing that Dolly was the one who had taken you was as close as Sheeley ever got to you. I don't think we'll ever know how he knew that. He never made any connection with Susan at all, as nearly as I can tell.''

"Yes, but Dolly must have been afraid he was going to.''

"Maria said he was asking about other people Dolly had worked for, so Dolly must have feared that he would eventually turn up Susan.''

"And the San Carlos Court?''

"My guess is that Maria Rivers's grandson, Johnny, suggested the San Carlos Court to Sheeley. If Sheeley had talked him into finding out where Dolly's phone calls were coming from with that special code the phone company has now and it had come back with just a pay phone number, Sheeley could have asked Johnny if he knew where that was. Johnny may have made up the part about the San Carlos Court so he could get money from Sheeley. He's been looking at a San Carlos Court postcard all his life. Or maybe she actually called from the San Carlos Court. She liked the place.''

"But how would Sheeley have recognized Dolly if he'd never met her before?''

"We can ask Maria, but my guess is that Dolly and Teresa looked alike, just like your mother and your aunt Lucy, not to mention you. He knew what Teresa looked like, and if he was expecting to find Dolly there, it wouldn't have been too difficult for him to recognize her.''

"And the fact that she was there was just a coincidence.''

"A coincidence, but things were sort of coming to a head anyway, or at least Dolly thought so. Maria told Dolly that Sheeley was looking for people she had worked for in the past. I think Dolly was afraid that he would eventually pick up on the Franklin connection and Susan; that's what her note was referring to. And because you had been on television. She couldn't protect you if you were going to become a celebrity; you look just like Paula. No wonder she got so upset when she saw you.''

FROM THERE, we headed south to Mount Vernon, where Maria was expecting us.

As before, Teresa met us at the door. I was a little

nervous about confronting them, considering what had happened to their little family since the last time I saw them. Far from blaming me for what had happened to Johnny, Maria and Teresa both apologized profusely for what he had done to me while they busied themselves, Teresa making the coffee and Maria arranging Tally's bouquet in a vase.

"For money he went and got his Aunt Dolly killed, and for money he would have got you killed, too," Maria spat, once we had finally sat down with our coffee. "We are ashamed that he was of our flesh and blood."

"I'm sure he didn't know what the consequences would be," I said soothingly.

Maria turned to me and said, without emotion, "Not to himself, that's for sure. We knew what a little weasel he was—we just didn't have any idea that he was capable of so much evil. He killed my daughter and Teresa's sister just as much as that old man did, and he was going to kill you, too. We'll talk no more of him."

There was a strong note of finality in that last statement; I had been so fascinated by the resolve in Maria's face while she made this speech that I hadn't looked at Teresa. When I was finally released from the momentary spell Maria cast, I looked at Teresa. She was nodding solemnly, indicating accord with her mother. If any tears were being shed for Johnny, it wasn't going to happen in front of us. At that moment I realized I was witnessing the genetic forces that had caused Dolly to keep her resolve for three decades.

"And so this is the beautiful baby that my Dolly saved," Maria said then, turning her beaming attention to Tally.

"Yes, I'm afraid so," Tally said.

"Don't say that. Dolly had a beautiful life and most of it was very happy. She only regretted that she couldn't be with us more. If she died fulfilling her mission of protecting you, she went straight to heaven."

We sat for an hour or so, drinking coffee and telling the Rivers women what we knew or could conjecture about our mutual histories. I didn't like to think that from now on the twenty-seventh of each month would come and go with no phone call, but there was nothing to be done about that.

From Mount Vernon, we went on to New Rochelle without speaking much. We each needed to absorb the impact of the scene we had just left. When we got to the Baker house, I left Tally by the car while I went to the door. This time Lucy answered the doorbell in person.

"Oh, it's you," she said with a little snarl, pointedly latching the screen door that separated us. "We called the *New Yorker*, you know. They'd never heard of you and they'd never heard of Catherine Christiansen, either. No one has ever heard of Catherine Christiansen. I don't know what it is you are trying to pull, but it won't work here."

"I came to apologize about that. If you'll let me explain, I think you'll understand. I did come to find out what I could about your sister, but not for the reason I told you. I know this will come as a shock, but your sister had a baby, a daughter, just before she died. That's why you hadn't seen her in so long. She didn't want you to know, or at least not yet."

"Now what kind of a scam are you pulling? You'd better leave, or I'm calling the police."

"You can certainly do that, and I can give you the names of police officers in Larchmont and a district attorney in White Plains that the New Rochelle police can contact who will verify what I'm telling you.''

This seemed to mollify her a little. At least she spared me a repeat of the lecture that Paula was not ''that kind'' of girl. I could only wonder if she had always suspected the reason for Paula's long absence.

''Well, what do you want from me?'' she said.

''I want you to meet your niece, Paula's daughter.''

''Is that the person you say is Paula's daughter?'' she said, pointing at Tally standing by the car.

''Yes.''

She wasn't ready yet to admit this possibility, so she unlatched the screen door and came out rather than inviting us in, and walked down the front walk. The resemblance to Paula must have worked its magic, because when she got close enough, she looked at Tally for a long moment and then took her in a warm embrace. I stood on the porch and watched.

They came up the walk together arm-in-arm.

''Now are you going to tell me why you gave us all that crap about Catherine what's-her-name last week?'' Lucy said to me.

''Sure. There aren't any secrets any more.''

We spent several hours with the Bakers telling them the story and letting them get acquainted with Tally.

MOLLY AND I flew home on Sunday. Molly was a seasoned traveler by now and treated the whole experience with a distinctively terrier nonchalance. Charlie had asked me to stay longer, but he seemed to understand when I said I needed to go home. It didn't seem likely to either of us that this would be our last meeting.

Boulder struck me as serene after the last month. No one could have asked for a quieter place to be that

Sunday afternoon when Molly and I crested the last hill and looked across the Boulder Valley to the Continental Divide.

So far, the media hadn't picked up much about the arrest for fraud and conspiracy of a high-profile society matron in Larchmont, but we figured it was only a matter of time and concluded that the right thing to do was to give Hank Sterling's organization their much-deserved scoop about the finding of a long-lost heiress. After all, without Celie Johnson I'd still be flailing around guessing at who Tally's father—if not her mother, as well—might be.

Once back in Boulder, I had two more phone calls I needed to make. The first was to Wes, to tell him where this whole story had wound up—I had forgotten him in the rush of events and, as far as he knew, I was still chasing around after ancient Westchester high school girls.

My second call was to Gladys, the mutual friend who had brought me together with the Richards so many years earlier.

Gladys was entranced by my story.

"The one thing that really bothers me about this whole thing," I said, "is that Susan gave me the proof of Tally's parentage, but never told me what it signified. It was only sheerest luck that I was able to identify Paula."

"Well, it was hardly luck that made you find her; it was talent and persistence," Gladys, always my most enthusiastic booster, said.

"Yes, but how could Susan believe that I could figure it out enough to do that?"

"The ring is all she gave you?" Gladys asked. "Did you look in the second compartment?"

"The second compartment?"

"Yes, that jewelry box has two hidden compartments. I was with her when she bought it up in Menlo Park, at that artisan's workshop place, and she was so delighted with it because it had the two compartments. She kept saying how perfect it was, because no one who found the first compartment would think to look for a second."

"Well she was right about that. Where is the second compartment?"

"Which one did you find, the small boxy one or the big flat one?"

"The small boxy one."

"Okay, the other one is under a false bottom in the big section of the top tray. It's very thin, it could only hold a few sheets of paper."

"Hold on," I said, and dug the jewelry box out of my still-packed luggage.

I quickly found a place where I could pry up the bottom of the section with a nail file. Inside was a note, covering two pages with Susan's precise and elegant handwriting. It was addressed to me. I read it aloud to Gladys.

Dearest Lexy,

If you are reading this note, it means that Peter and I are no longer able to protect Tally and it is now up to you. I haven't told you this before because the fewer people who know it, the safer Tally is.

There are ruthless people who would destroy Tally rather than let her be reunited with her natural family. For that reason, Peter and I have decided to keep the circumstances of her birth secret, even from her. The information here is in case you should determine that it is necessary or desirable to rethink that decision. Tally's natural parents, both of whom died shortly after she was born, were Paula Jordan Chandler of White Plains and Lawrence Foster Prescott III of Larchmont. Tally's grandfather is Lawrence Foster Prescott II of Larchmont.

A friend of mine, a nurse named Dolly Rivers who once took care of my mother, was caring for Tally when Tally's parents died in what was called an accident.

Dolly knows that it was not an accident—she saw them leave together in the same car instead of being in two different cars as the accident was reported, and someone else was driving the other car. But Dolly has no way of proving this and she has always been afraid if she revealed where Tally was, the people responsible for Tally's parents' deaths would also harm Tally.

Dolly knew that Peter and I were moving to California and asked if she and Tally could come with us until it was safe for Tally to be taken to her grandfather. During that trip we decided that Tally would be safer with us than with Dolly.

Dolly believes that Tally is still in danger and, to this day, reports an ongoing effort to find her and Tally from people she believes would do Tally harm. There is a considerable fortune involved but we have provided for Tally's financial future and we don't believe any fortune is worth the risk.

Dolly says that the ring with the blue stone (in the other secret compartment) will prove who

Tally is to her grandfather, if necessary. Dolly, whose last name is now Miller, lives in Santa Barbara and can provide other details if they are needed.

Here's hoping you never have to do anything about this, but somebody has to know just in case.

All my love,
Susan

P.S. And you always thought we were so square!

"See," Gladys laughed, "Susan didn't think you were so damned smart after all."

"When I think of all the time I spent thinking that ring was a clue and running around asking strangers about lost rings—it's a good thing I didn't know that it didn't mean anything when I started. And it's a good thing Paula Chandler didn't go to high school in Nebraska."

"'When ignorance is bliss, 'tis folly to be wise,'" she quoted, and made me laugh.

"Well, hardly bliss in this case. But Susan should have told me something about it. Imagine if we'd never even thought of looking in the jewelry box," I complained.

"I'm sure she was planning to tell you. None of us expect to die when we're only forty-eight—she thought she had all kinds of time to let you know. In any case, I know she's glad she gave *you* the jewelry box. She was a very wise woman, our Susan."

EPILOGUE

In April of the following year, I had a phone call.

"Lexy?"

"Wes! How's it going?"

"Just fine, just fine. I just came from a meeting with the producers and they love the script."

"Well, good. I'm glad to hear it."

"Yeah, they just wanted a few changes."

"Don't they always?"

"Yeah, well I thought you'd want to know."

"Sounds ominous. What did they do?"

"Well, they made you a little younger. They said you just weren't believable as a character. And there's only one TV actress in town who could play you as written."

"Only one that's fat enough, right."

"They didn't actually say that, but it was pretty obvious that's what they meant. It was worth a shot— you keep hoping things will change. As a matter of principle, they get all pissy when writers try to control character descriptions. We're not supposed to inhibit the creative process by telling them the heroine is blond. Anyway, they're thinking of Tara Shields for the part. And the dog is going to be a collie; the producer's wife breeds collies."

"I suppose that's better than making me a guy, but Molly won't like it at all."

"Actually, they thought about making you a guy, but they already have this three-picture deal with Tara and the Tally part isn't big enough for Tara. They're going to give Tara a love interest with the LA detective, instead.''

"Oh, Bruce Morita's going to love that. What else?''

"Well, they scrapped the heiress angle—said it was too old-fashioned. They think it's better if they're after the girl because of a mob vendetta. She's the daughter of a squealer.''

"So it is the DNA after all.''

"What?''

"Oh, nothing—just a private joke between Tally and me. They put in a chase scene, too, didn't they?''

"Well, that's not final yet. They may move the eastern location to Miami. The studio has good connections with a local shooting unit there. And in Miami, they can do a chase scene with boats and helicopters if they want to. Everybody thought that was a terrific idea.''

"What else?''

"Hey, they're keeping all the dogs, and everybody in my agent's office was betting that the dogs would have to go.''

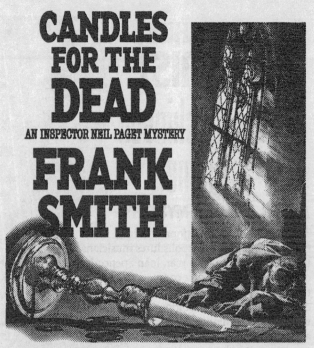

CANDLES FOR THE DEAD

AN INSPECTOR NEIL PAGET MYSTERY

FRANK SMITH

A woman is found bludgeoned to death in St. Justin's Church. Detective Chief Inspector Neil Paget and Sergeant John Tregalles probe Beth Smallwood's life and discover a world of tragedy, violence and ugly secrets. Who could have killed her in such a brutal fashion?

Was it the son she was ready to turn over to the police? The fellow employee who'd lost his promotion to Beth? Paget cleverly uncovers the missing pieces as he confronts the third anniversary of his wife's death and the demons that still torment him. With Tregalles by his side, the duo close in on an unexpected killer.

Available October 2000 at your favorite retail outlet.

WORLDWIDE LIBRARY®

WFS363

SIMON BRETT

Mrs. Pargeter's Point of Honour

A MRS. PARGETER MYSTERY

While activities of her dearly departed husband often
took place beyond the confines of the law, the genteel
Mrs. Pargeter considers it a point of honour to resolve
any unfinished business he left behind.

Veronica Chastaigne, widow to one of Mr. Pargeter's
partners in crime, is anxious to return her gallery of
priceless "borrowed" paintings to their rightful owners.
Graciously accommodating, Mrs. P. assembles her husband's
cast of merry crooks to smuggle a fortune in Rembrandts and
da Vincis out of England. But a caper worthy of dear Mr. P.
wouldn't be up to snuff without the challenges of a bumbling
inspector, a mysterious informant and a crafty interloper who
manages to steal the paintings first....

Available September 2000
at your favorite retail outlet.

NORDIC NIGHTS

AN ALIX THORSSEN MYSTERY

Lise McClendon

The wealthy resort town of Jackson Hole, Wyoming, is knee-deep in ice and snow, but winter is a thriving season for gallery owner Alix Thorssen. Glasius Dokken's talent as an artist makes him a Swedish national treasure, and thanks to Alix, he's brought his Viking murals for the annual Nordic Nights Festival. Unfortunately, murder steals the show.

When the artist is found dead, Alix's own stepfather, Hank, is jailed as the prime suspect. Soon, Alix is unraveling a complex web of greed, deception and misplaced loyalty in the frigid, icy landscapes, which are at once surreal and deadly.

Available October 2000
at your favorite retail outlet.

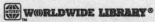
WORLDWIDE LIBRARY®

WLM364

THE SECRET IS OUT!

HARLEQUIN®

INTRIGUE®

presents

**By day these agents are cowboys;
by night they are specialized
government operatives.
Men bound by love, loyalty and the law—
they've vowed to keep their missions
and identities confidential....**

Harlequin Intrigue

HARLEQUIN®

Makes any time special ™